THERE MUST BE SOMETHING MORE

Carol
Clancy

Order this book online at www.trafford.com
or email orders@trafford.com

Most Trafford titles are also available at major online book retailers.

Printed in Victoria, BC, Canada.

ISBN: 978-1-4269-2786-7

Library of Congress Control Number: 2010910313

*Our mission is to efficiently provide the world's finest, most comprehensive book publishing
service, enabling every author to experience success. To find out how to publish your book, your
way, and have it available worldwide, visit us online at www.trafford.com*

Trafford rev. 7/12/2010

 www.trafford.com

North America & international
toll-free: 1 888 232 4444 (USA & Canada)
phone: 250 383 6864 ♦ fax: 812 355 4082

In loving memory of Sully

(Any resemblance to the character of
Barney Fife is purely coincidental.)

Chapter One

What I've never been able to understand is how long it takes people to die. It can take weeks, months, years of lingering somewhere in between life and death. I always wanted to say to them—just go, get the hell out of here. But that, of course, was not my job.

And so I would sit patiently with them, like I did with Mrs. Avery that day, murmuring things like, "It's okay to let go," as if she needed my permission. She seemed to need someone's permission; it might as well have been mine. Mrs. Avery gave no response, of course. She continued to lie still in her hospital bed, the bars pulled up next to her, her white hair pulled back from her blank face. Machines surrounded her on every side, not exactly keeping her alive, but not allowing her to die either. The room was quiet, with just the slight hum of the equipment and the raspy sound of Mrs. Avery's slow, shallow breathing.

The nurse came in as I sat there, patting Mrs. Avery's hand through the metal bar. She smiled at me as she checked Mrs. Avery's vitals, and I smiled back, as if this were the most fulfilling moment I'd ever had. But all I could think was—don't do this, Mrs. Avery. Don't make life so unbearable. Don't gasp for breath and twitch your arm and never open your eyes. Don't make me think that this is all there is.

With one last pat, I stood up and began the long walk back to my office. The nursing home was all on one level, so even though it was not a large building, the walk from one end to the other seemed long. The strong scent of antiseptic mixed with the smells of urine and sweat and death, causing that particularly strong odor everyone always complains about in

1

nursing homes. It was oddly comforting to me now, though, as I walked. The theme song of *Little House on the Prairie* mingled with shouts of "Five-ninety-nine" from *The Price is Right* and the cheerful voice of the physical therapist calling out, "Now, lift your arm, Mr. Vanderbilt."

One of the aides stopped me on the way and told me that Mrs. Johnson in Room 306 needed new shoes.

"What size?" I asked.

"Oh, I don't know. A 7 or 7 ½. It doesn't really matter since she can't walk anyway."

"I'll get them today," I told her and started on.

"Oh, and Nora," she called out, "Mrs. Lander's lock is jammed."

I paused. "Am I supposed to do something about it?"

"Well, I don't know who else to tell. And since you're the social worker—"

"I'll look into it," I told her, hopelessness overwhelming me. It was all too much for a twenty-five-year-old. I was supposed to be making a difference. I was supposed to be doing something meaningful. And instead I was talking to people who couldn't hear me and buying shoes for people who couldn't walk and fixing door locks that people would never use.

I sank into the chair in my office, finally alone. My office was like a small closet near the front of the building. Everything in it was fairly new—the desk, the chair, the computer, the phone, even the tile on the floor. I put pictures on the wall and a live plant on the desk that I had to replace every month because there was no natural light. But a fake plant wouldn't work, not here. The office had no windows, but it did have a door. A door that closed.

But that didn't always work.

"Nora," a voice on the intercom came through, the buzzing almost as loud as the voice. "New patient arriving."

I sighed. I worked in a small nursing home with only about sixty patients, but that meant they were all mine. And everything that went along with them was all mine. Whether it was buying shoes or fixing door locks or helping to check them in. All of it fell to me, the twenty-five-year-old social worker who was going to change the world.

I went down to the desk to pick up the paperwork on the new patient. I passed Mr. Halloran on the way.

"Hey, baby," he said. "You sure are looking good today. Mmm, mmm."

"Hello, Mr. Halloran," I said, ignoring his comment. If only it were possible to sue a forgetful seventy-year-old in a wheelchair for sexual harassment. But I knew no court would side with me. Even if I told them that Mr. Halloran was a retired construction worker. Even if I told them that he had once pinched the butt of a very respectable, middle-aged woman who had leaned over to kiss her mother hello, not realizing that frail Mr. Halloran sitting behind her in his wheelchair was any kind of threat. The woman had jumped about two feet and looked back at Mr. Halloran with a slightly horrified, slightly pleased expression on her face. I was sure she had not been approached that way in a very long time. But I knew that Mr. Halloran would always fall back on his senility as his defense, and if that didn't work, his lengthy lists of medications would do it. I had no chance in any court.

The paperwork was the usual. But this time it was another MS patient, a woman in her forties who could no longer live at home. I stood for a long moment staring at the forms, all signed illegibly.

"Nora?" I looked up to see Jean, the receptionist, watching me.

"Okay," I said, pretending nothing was wrong. "I'm on my way."

I walked as normally as I could, right past Mr. Halloran smacking his lips. I turned to my right, past my office, and smiled at an Alzheimer's patient passing me. We must have looked like a reflection of each other, my face as blank as hers. I just made it to the bathroom, leaning against the door as the waves of nausea flowed through me.

I couldn't do it. I couldn't face another patient like this. All I could see was Susan McDonald's face—our last M.S. patient—her eyes rolling in her head as she told me how Jesus loved her and Jesus loved me and it would all work out in the end. She had come in completely paralyzed from her disease, her hands and feet curling up, her face twitching. When I interviewed her on her first day, taking her "social history," she had stressed over and over that she was a Christian and how grateful she was for Jesus' love. She was only thirty-three when she came in, and turned thirty-four before she died. There were seven agonizing months of Jesus' love before she'd finally succumbed to pneumonia.

I glanced at the paperwork in my hand. Maggie Applebaum, forty-two years old, diagnosed with MS ten years ago, no longer functionally independent. Functionally independent? I thought. Was anyone functionally independent?

I washed my face with cold water and looked at myself in the mirror. My pale skin was even paler than usual. My dark brown layers that were supposed to be falling casually around my face in soft swirls seemed to be sticking straight out from my head. I pulled on them, trying to rearrange them, but it was no use. The one advantage to working here was that no one would notice.

I patted my cheekbones, trying to bring out some color, smiled, and did my best to look chipper. "Miss Social Worker," I called myself sometimes. It was like a very bad part in a play. Or at least, I was playing the part very badly. I couldn't figure out which one it was.

I walked slowly to Maggie Applebaum's room. Harriet, another Alzheimer's patient passed me, clapping her hands compulsively as she often did. "Good for you! Good for you!" she said over and over. I had to smile at that.

Maggie was sitting in her wheelchair when I walked into her room. Her short, dark hair was streaked with gray, and she was unnaturally thin and wiry, which made her face look older than she was. She wore jeans and a baggy t-shirt, as if she were on her way to the grocery store or bank, only running errands and not bothering much with the way she looked.

"Hello," she said. "What's so funny?"

"Oh," I said, not realizing I was still smiling. I hesitated. "It's just that sometimes you get encouragement in the strangest ways," I said finally, thinking of Harriet.

"I know what you mean," she agreed.

I pulled out a chair and sat across from her.

"So tell me about yourself," she said.

I was startled. "Umm, well—" I wasn't sure what to say. "I think I'm supposed to be asking you that."

She laughed. "I know. I'm just so sick of being interviewed by people. No offense, but doctors, and nurses, and I'm assuming you're some kind of activity director or something. You look so young. I just couldn't resist rattling you a little."

"I'm the social worker," I said, maybe just a little defensively.

"I'm sorry. I didn't have you pegged as someone so important."

I had to laugh again. It would have been nice to have made it through at least one day without being thrown off guard. That was the problem with my part in this play. It never went the way it was scripted.

Maggie seemed to read my mind. "I'm sorry," she said. "Let's start again. Actually, you start, since I think that's the way it's supposed to work."

"Hello," I said, sticking out my hand to shake hers. I could see that her fingers were slightly bent when they met mine.

"I'm Nora Sullivan, the social worker here at Longate Nursing Home. I'd like to welcome you to our lovely accommodations and make sure you're finding everything you need."

"Well," she said approvingly. "Aren't you Miss Social Worker?"

I stared at her.

"What's the matter?"

"I just, uhh, I was just thinking the exact same thing before I came in here. I mean I call myself that sometimes, kind of as my own inside joke." I felt myself blushing at how stupid I must sound.

"Well, there you go," she said. "You're right. You are Miss Social Worker."

I smiled at her. "Okay," I said. "You threw me off again."

"I'm sorry. I have the worst habit of doing that to people. Go ahead."

"*Are* you settling in okay?" I asked lamely.

"Yes, these first fifteen minutes have gone smashingly. The best place I've ever been. I do have one question, however."

"Go ahead," I said, playing along with her sarcasm.

She nodded over towards her roommate, one of our patients that could be said to be well—lingering somewhere between life and death. Another semi-comatose state, I guess you could say.

"I know she won't be speaking to me. But can she hear everything?"

I hesitated. "I don't really know," I told her. "I like to think she can hear, that she has some awareness, but I don't think anyone really knows."

"You *like* to think that she has some awareness?" She looked horrified. "What an awful state to be in."

"Well, I don't really mean I'd like that to be true." I stopped. This was going very badly. "I just don't know. When I speak to her, I'd like to think on some level she can hear me, but of course, I wouldn't want her to be suffering or be trapped in that state. I guess I'm talking about different levels of awareness."

She seemed intrigued by that. I was quite intrigued myself. I had never put my thoughts about all of it into words before.

"Hmm. I like that idea much better. 'On some level.' We do have different levels of awareness, don't we?"

"I guess so," I agreed. I pulled out my clipboard, hoping we could get back to a more official introduction to the nursing home.

"You're probably wondering why I care," she said. "As if my husband and I might be having wild sex and want to make sure she can't hear anything. You're thinking something like that, right?"

I cleared my throat. This was not a conversation I was used to having at work. "I can't say I was thinking that, no."

She was smiling at me. "Good," she said. "I wouldn't want you to get the wrong idea about me." We both began to laugh.

"Okay," I said. "We really have to do this the right way."

"I understand," she said. "Go ahead."

I looked down at the information I had on her. There was a series of questions I needed to ask her about her life before coming to the nursing home. It was a way we got to know our patients so that we could serve them better. That kind of thing.

"So these are questions we ask all our patients when they arrive," I told her.

"Aren't we called residents?"

"Oh God," I said. I always forgot that. I think it was because it seemed like the most subtle of lies. You could pretend like you were going on a cruise or staying in a hotel, when in fact you were checking into a place to die. That fact alone made it a hard word for me to remember.

"You're trying to torture me, right?" I asked her, not explaining my most current theory to her. Levels of awareness were one thing. Coming here to die was another.

She smiled. "What else am I going to do with my time?"

"Okay, you win. These are questions we ask all our new *residents.*"

"Much better," she murmured.

"So you're Maggie Applebaum, you're forty-two years old and—" I hesitated.

"What brings me here?"

"Well, yeah, that's one way of putting it."

She began to tell me the short version of her life, as they all did. Whether I talked to patients (residents) or their families, they all told me about as much as you would expect someone to tell a complete stranger. Sometimes angry or hurt family members would begin to tell me too much, how their father had "always been nothin' but a son-of-a-bitch," or their mother had been "essentially self-centered her entire life." Or maybe it was an aunt or an uncle being checked in who had no one else, and the family resented having to care for them. It was intimate information that I really had no right to know, yet since I was asking . . .

What I had come to understand about people from these social histories, even from the ones that gave me only the most superficial information, is that when we get old we only become more of what we've always been. We like to think that we change, that people only become crotchety and outspoken, or maybe wise and mellow, in their old age. But the truth is whatever we have been is what we will be, only magnified. That is what I had come to know about getting old, even at my young age.

But it was the younger patients who I had no theories for, the ones whose lives fell apart in a moment, or maybe in a series of moments. We had one patient who had been in a motorcycle accident at twenty-five, a woman in her forties who had a stroke and could no longer remember her name, and worst of all for me, the few MS patients who had come in and slowly watched their bodies, and sometimes their minds, deteriorate.

Maggie now began to tell me briefly about her early life, being the oldest of three children, going to college, getting a job in the corporate world. "The typical suburban life," she called it.

"I was diagnosed when I was about thirty," Maggie told me. "Right after I got married." I could feel her looking at me as I diligently took notes, my head down.

"You can keep going," I said as I wrote.

"Okay, I just don't want you to miss anything." I realized maybe I should be more actively involved and lifted my head up.

She was smiling. "I bet you were the best student in the class."

"I'm sorry," I said. "Go ahead."

"I'm sure you've heard it before," she continued. "It started with the small things, you know, stumbling, dropping things. I went through a series of tests. At first, they hoped it might be something else, something 'less problematic' as one doctor so elegantly put it, but of course, as we can see now, it's become a bit problematic." She paused. "The first years were not so bad. Episodes here and there, but I always got better again. The last few years have been rough."

"I'm sorry," I mumbled. I looked at my notes. "Do you have any children?" I asked.

"No," she said. "I followed my doctor's advice not to have any."

"And your parents, brothers or sisters?"

"My father died about five years ago," she said. "My mother just left about ten minutes ago, but will probably be visiting regularly. My brother and sister are out of town but send Hallmark as often as they can."

7

I wasn't sure if she was being sarcastic or not on that last point. "And your husband," I said, looking around the room as if he might have been hiding in the bathroom all this time. "Is he here today?"

"No," she said. "He's at work."

I was confused. That seemed a little strange on the day his wife was admitted to a nursing home.

"Will he be here later then?" I asked.

She sighed. "My husband is a lovely man," she said finally. "But he's not taking this well. I know—you're thinking, after twelve years, he's just now finding out he can't handle it?"

I didn't know what to say. Did she want me to answer the question? But she answered it herself.

"He's always been one for delayed reactions. He just can't deal with this." She spread her arms around her as if to take in the room, the semi-comatose roommate, the hospital bed, her wheelchair, my presence, anything that might be included in how far down she had gone. "He's leaving me."

"I'm sorry," I mumbled again.

"Look," she said, peering at me closely as if she were deeply concerned. "You seem to be taking this harder than I am right now." I realized my face must be showing the horror I was feeling.

"No, I'm fine," I said. "But I guess I should be moving on to some other things I need to get done. Is there anything I can get you?"

She patted my hand. "It will be okay," she said, almost in a maternal manner. I stood up.

"I'll be back in to see you soon," I said. "And of course the nurse can get you anything you need."

Maggie was chuckling softly. I couldn't imagine what she could possibly be finding so funny right now.

I walked out the door and stood for a moment in the hallway next to her room, clutching Maggie's chart to my chest as if it were all I had to hold onto. Could there be a more embarrassing moment for "Miss Social Worker" than an MS patient comforting me over her disease? I didn't think so.

I could see Mr. Halloran slowly pushing his way towards me. "Hey honey," he was calling. "You sure are looking good today."

Damn, I thought, can't he even remember that he just used that line an hour ago? "I'll see you tomorrow, Mr. Halloran," I said. "I've got to run now."

Chapter Two

It was such a relief to come home to Barney Fife.

People always asked me, "How could you have named your dog that?" As if I'd given my child some horrible name like Constantine or Elmer that would scar him for life. But Barney Fife couldn't be scarred for life by his name; that was the whole point.

My friend Sharon had found him wandering the streets as a puppy and couldn't keep him. Then he was just this small yellow thing, a lab mix we thought, though we didn't really know anything about dogs. But he was the dopiest puppy when I met him. He looked up at me with these huge eyes that seemed to understand absolutely nothing, and he fell over himself trying to get me to pet him. Then when I took him for a walk around the block on a leash, he walked ahead of me with such unwarranted confidence. He would bark at other dogs as if he owned the block, and try to chase squirrels and chipmunks as if he were the head of some sort of small animal police squad, charged with ridding the neighborhood of all pests.

"He reminds me of Barney Fife," I told Sharon. Both Sharon and I loved watching old reruns of *Andy Griffith* on TV Land. We'd compare notes on Aunt Bea and Gomer Pyle. But most of all we loved Barney Fife's bravado. And so that was it; my dog had his name.

Since that time, over a year ago, little Barney Fife had grown into a much bigger dog, about 70 pounds. And of course the dopey thing was all just a big act. He still came across as a dim-witted, over-confident fool, but I had come to realize it was all just a plot to get the world to underestimate him. While you were laughing at him and thinking yourself so superior to him, he was busy molding the world and its people to his exact specifications.

So when I came home every night from Longate Nursing Home, Barney would bark his command at me, and we'd go out in the yard for him to do his business. I lived in the garage apartment of a suburban house that was built in the early 1900s. It had one of those really strange set-ups that these kinds of places sometimes have—a large kitchen, but a small bedroom, with the bathroom off the bedroom. It wasn't a large apartment, but not small either. I guess you could say it was a little eccentric. But it suited Barney Fife and me just fine since I guess you could say we were both a little eccentric too.

But the yard behind the house was not really big enough for Barney, as he let me know right from the start by chewing apart first my couch, then my chair, and finally, my bathroom tile. It was then that I realized Barney Fife needed a bigger world to explore. And every day, we would go out exploring that world together.

That night after Barney's walk, dinner, four cookies, and doggie ice cream, he finally decided my duties were done for the evening and settled on the couch, just above the hole he had dug in it.

"Okay, Barney," I said. "I'm sorry to leave you again, but I have to go to my class tonight." He looked up at me with a slightly mystified expression, one that said—I don't really care, but I guess you're going to tell me anyway. He rolled over on his side, and I patted his belly. I did hate to leave him after a full day at work, but there was no other choice. I had my class to go to. And I was sure it was going to be good for both of us eventually.

I was taking what was called a "Prosperity Class" at a local church I'd been hanging around, though not really joining. I'd started going to the church about a month ago, though I wasn't sure why, and I'd seen a sign for the class hanging in the foyer. Let's just say as a social worker making barely above minimum wage, the sign caught my attention.

"Barney," I told him as I left. "If all goes as planned, you'll have more doggy bones than you know what to do with." I thought I heard a grunt of acknowledgement as I closed the door, but it could have been my imagination.

I made it to the class a few minutes late. It was held in a room in the back of the church at the end of a long hall. This was one of those modern churches with plenty of classrooms and extra space for a bookstore and party room, all of the amenities any group of spiritual people could possibly need.

It was only the second class, and the instructor was still going over the basics as I walked in. Last week he had told us that we needed to start saying "I am prosperous" one hundred times a day. I hadn't done it. I couldn't think of anything more stupid than that. I was hoping that this week he would come up with another exercise, one that actually made sense.

But instead, as I sat down, I heard people giving examples of how well it had worked. One woman had received a $100 check in the mail. A salesman in the group had a great week. Another woman found her lost wedding ring. And on and on they went. I tried to resist rolling my eyes. Ed, the instructor, was very enthusiastic. He was a tall, slim man with hair that was thinning and bags under his eyes. I couldn't be sure how old he was, but he had been involved with the church for ten years, and it had completely transformed his life, as he told it.

"Nora," Ed finally said, trying to include me since I was late. "Do you have any examples?"

I was starting to get a little nervous. "Is there a psychological theory behind all of this?" I asked instead.

"You're changing your thinking. That's the theory. Remember—what you think about is what you create."

"Hmm," I mumbled. "I guess I was expecting a little something different from this class."

"What were you expecting?" Ed asked.

"Well," I hesitated. What was I going to say? Something less stupid? "I guess I thought we would talk about some better ways to make money."

"That's a good point, Nora," Ed said, trying to pretend that it really was. "Sometimes we think prosperity is about what we do, when really it's about what we think." He went on, then, to explain how our thinking creates our reality. Much of the same stuff he had said last week. I sighed. We weren't going to be moving on to another topic, as I had hoped. We weren't going to be talking about how I could find a job that actually paid me a lot of money to do meaningful work instead of one that paid me almost nothing to have almost no effect on the world. I was depressed.

The class let out after about an hour, and I wandered into the lobby of the church. I looked around, and just as I had hoped, I found who I was looking for. I guess it wasn't exactly true that I wasn't sure why I was going to this new church. It might have had something to do with Frank. He was a guy I'd been seeing for about a month, a guy I'd met in a bar of all places, who had invited me to his New Age church. That was the great thing about New Age religion. You could meet a church-going guy in a bar.

"Frank," I said, and he turned away from his conversation with someone. Every time I saw him, it struck me how good looking he was, with dark curly hair, olive skin, and a big grin he liked to flash at you to throw you off guard. He was beyond confident in his abilities to charm, in his knowledge and intelligence, in just about everything. That was what I think attracted me the most. But I couldn't figure out what he was doing with me.

"Nora," he said with a gust of enthusiasm as he me gave me a big hug. That was the other thing about New Age religion I'd come to realize. Feelings were always enthusiastic, even when they were forced.

"So, how did the class go?"

"Well," I hesitated yet again. "It was great." The forced enthusiasm never seemed to work as well for me. He caught on right away.

"I really think you need to stay open-minded," he said. "There's a lot you can learn. There's a reason you were drawn to that class."

"Yeah," I mumbled as he turned to say another enthusiastic hello to a woman walking by. "It's called poverty."

"What?" he asked turning back to me, but still holding onto the arm of the woman he was talking to, as if he were afraid she would get away. I could tell it was me who needed to get away.

"I've got to go," I said. "You know, Barney and all that."

I thought I noticed a slight eye roll, but he covered it well. Frank was not someone who understood the joys of dog ownership.

"Okay, tell the big guy I said hello. Are we still on for Saturday?"

"Of course," I said, as I started walking out. "I'll be there at seven."

I was going to listen to his band play at a bar, the same one I'd met him at. He hadn't been singing that night, but he had told me his band played there occasionally. Finally, I was going to go hear them play.

It was incredible, really, I thought now as I walked to my car. How I had managed to meet a musician. He was perfect for me. Good looking, creative, fun, and yet something else I couldn't quite name. Something that always made me uncomfortable. I tried to shake it off, as I always did, and yet there it was again.

When I got home, Barney was up from his after-dinner nap and waiting for me.

"Okay," I sighed and grabbed his leash. He bounded over to me and tried to wait patiently as I attached it. But it was nearly impossible for him to manage.

"Barney," I said as his collar moved every time I got close to clicking the leash in place. "You have to sit still!" My sternness had no effect on him, but finally I was able to catch the hook as it circled around my hand. We both ran down the steps together. I figured it was easier than trying to pretend I could slow him down.

We walked the dark streets as we did almost every night. It was early spring, and the air was cool, with a crisp breeze that carried the scent of someone's fireplace burning. I tightened my jacket around me and looked up at the stars. I could make out only a few in the dark night, as if the sky was trying to be overcast but not quite making it. Barney was alert, focused, and intent on stopping every ten seconds to smell the grass. It drove me crazy.

We arrived at the nearby schoolyard, and Barney's ears perked up as soon as he saw his Rottweiler friend. We often ran into the dog and his owner around this time of night. They would be walking through the parking lot coming from the back, just as we were approaching. For Barney, it was like he had finally found his soul mate. Barney was close to 70 pounds, but this Rottweiler was probably 120 pounds. Barney would approach him with unbridled joy, pulling me along with him as he ran up to him, and then he would let loose—jumping over him and under him and around him. Sometimes it looked like Barney was actually somersaulting over him, though he would do it so fast, I couldn't be sure, and I could never figure out how he landed on his feet. The whole time, the Rottweiler would stand, as if at attention, not moving a muscle. Not stopping Barney, but not joining him either. It was as if he were a wise, old soul who let Barney act out all his passion and just waited patiently for him to be through.

"Hey, Barney," the man said.

"Hi, Russo," I called to his dog.

I had never gotten the man's name. He had never asked for mine. It was strange, but I wasn't even sure what he looked like. I knew he had a beer gut and wore the same jean jacket almost every night. I could barely see his slightly puffy features in the dark and sometimes he seemed to have a day or two's growth of beard. But other than that I couldn't really see him. I could probably pass him in broad daylight and not even recognize him.

We followed the same pattern every time. We both laughed at Barney's antics. We commented on his dog's stoicism. He leaned down and scratched Barney's ears, and I gingerly patted his dog's head, getting about the same response that Barney got—nothing. I was never really sure what Barney saw in this dog, but then sometimes there really is no way to account for friendship, is there?

Finally, we said our goodbyes, and Barney and I continued our walk. I was debating with myself but then decided to give it a try.

"I am prosperous," I said out loud. It sounded strange. I looked around to make sure no one could hear me, but the streets were quiet. No one in sight.

"I am prosperous," I said again. I hesitated, and then shrugged. Well, what could it hurt?

I said it ten more times, and got very bored. I tried singing it. I tried whispering it. I lost track of how many times I actually said it. But I kept repeating it until we got back to the apartment.

"I am so damn prosperous," I said as we came in the door and I unsnapped Barney's leash. "And I hate this stupid class."

I realized Barney was looking at me with that look that said— what is she doing now? It was clear to me that as funny as I found Barney, he found me equally as humorous. As if he was never quite sure what to make of me. I wasn't always sure what to make of me either.

"You are prosperous, Barney," I said. He wagged his tail, so I repeated it again.

"You are soooo prosperous."

Chapter Three

At age ninety-nine, Mr. Gordon was our oldest resident at Longate Nursing Home. I could confidently call Mr. Gordon a "resident" because he had most certainly not come to the nursing home to die. Because of his considerable wealth, he was able to afford a private room, which he had fixed up to look like a small office/bedroom, more office than bedroom. The hospital bed was the only thing that gave away the fact that Mr. Gordon was in a healthcare facility, and even the bars on the bed somehow seemed to fit into the décor of a professor hard at work on his most recent research project.

I could hear the clack, clack of Mr. Gordon's manual typewriter as I knocked on the door.

He called for me to come in. Mr. Gordon was a small, wiry man. He was very short now, though he was stooped and probably shorter than he had been as a young man. He wore wire glasses that he constantly adjusted as he spoke, and somehow, incredibly, he still had a full head of thick, wavy white hair. None of us could figure out how that hair had lasted almost one hundred years.

He was hunched over his typewriter as I came in, and seemed deep in thought for a second, but then he suddenly burst into a crescendo of typing with two fingers until he came to a stop with a flourish of his hands, as if he were ending a passionate piano recital.

"Good morning, Mr. Gordon," I shouted. In spite of Mr. Gordon's incredible intellect, he unfortunately did not believe that he had a hearing problem and refused to wear a hearing aide. "Those crazy doctors don't know what they're talking about," was the way he put it. "They can't even be out of high school yet." To Mr. Gordon, everyone looked like they were either about to graduate from high school or had just gotten out. If you didn't look like you were even close to getting a diploma, he wouldn't listen to a word you said. I was, of course, one of the latter.

"Mr. Gordon," I shouted again. "We have these things called computers now. Why don't you let me look into getting you a nice used one?"

He waved his hand in front of his face. "Pfff," was all he said. I had tried before, but it was a hopeless cause. I think he enjoyed banging on his old manual too much. It looked like it couldn't have been made any later than 1920, but to him it was like a musical instrument, one he had primed and polished and molded to his own talented fingers. Nothing else would do.

"Did I tell you I'm working on my autobiography?" He had, several times, but I didn't mention it. "What is it that they call it these days?"

"Your memoirs," I said.

"Ah yes, memoirs," he said, pronouncing it like "memo wars."

"Sit down, sit down," he said, motioning to an armchair. He was without a doubt the only resident in the nursing home with a cushioned armchair. I sat on the edge of it, not allowing myself to get too comfortable.

Although in Mr. Gordon's eyes I was too young to have any knowledge myself, he did enjoy sharing his with me. It was an unequal exchange, one where he did all the talking and couldn't hear much of what I said in response anyway.

"Have I told you about the war?" he asked.

"Which one?" I asked warily.

"I'm often struck by the evil," he continued on as if I hadn't spoken. "The sheer evil of it all."

"Hitler?" I asked.

"Einstein," he responded.

"Einstein?"

"The atomic bomb," he said, as if I were the biggest idiot he'd ever met in his life. "It was Einstein who encouraged the United States to develop the atomic bomb."

He paused for dramatic effect. I waited. I couldn't figure out how Einstein played into Mr. Gordon's autobiography, but I was willing to stay open-minded.

"The choice he was given," he continued. "This was the one weapon that could destroy our planet. The evil it brought into the world." He shook his head in disbelief. "And yet Einstein was not an evil man. Oh no, far from it. He was a pacifist. Did you know that?"

"No," I admitted. We didn't study Einstein for a major in social work.

"The choice that he had to make was astounding. To continue to believe in pacifism when such evil is being done in the world. And then to ultimately choose what some might call an equally evil solution. Only Einstein could handle such a moral dilemma."

"Mr. Gordon," I said, trying to move things along. "How does this fit into your autobiography?"

"It was the social atmosphere of that time," he said again with utter disdain for my lack of understanding. "What we lived with then. You young people don't understand such moral dilemmas. You shoot each other because you don't like the way someone talks to you. You go to war over oil. Oh, I know," he said, holding up his hand as if I were arguing with him. "You don't call it that. But that's what it is, you know. You don't know the world we lived in then, the real choices we had to make."

I sat silently as his rant continued.

"Do you know we would sit around the kitchen table and discuss these things? That's right," he continued as if I had expressed my complete surprise. "We discussed the war and the choices our country had to make. Can you imagine you young people doing that these days? Ha! You're too busy watching those silly shows on television, those people singing and dancing and all of you calling in to make your choice on who is the best. Ha! We made real choices back then."

He paused. I knew better than to interrupt his train of thought. He was more pensive now, quieter, but equally intense. "You know the only way to fight such evil was to match that evil. It was the only way, and yet it was evil. Do you understand?" He looked at me unflinchingly.

I thought I did understand, but I didn't really want to.

"So you've made it to World War II in your book," I said, easing us back onto safer ground. "It sounds like it's coming along."

"World War II was essentially a continuation of World War I you see," he continued.

"Uh-huh."

"The world could not seem to sort out its issues." He chuckled as if he were talking about a mere family dispute. "So we had the war to end all wars, and then of course, it didn't end all wars. We only knew we needed the I after the II, you see."

"Was there any other social atmosphere at the time?" I asked loudly.

"Oh, my dear," he said in a tone that told me I understood absolutely nothing. "When there is a world war going on, there is hardly any other social atmosphere to speak of."

"What about in your own life?" I tried. "Was there anything else going on?"

He paused as if he were thinking it through. "No," he said finally. "I believe World War II was a true turning point in civilization."

I sighed. He obviously had not heard the question.

"It was a turning point because of the atomic bomb, you see."

"Uh-huh."

"We had to end the war, we had to do what it took to really finish them off, you see. Oh, but what a moral price we paid."

I did not know how much more of Mr. Gordon's moral price I could take. "Mr. Gordon, maybe you should include some personal aspects to your autobiography."

He waved his hand again. "It's all about the social context," he said. "Without the social context, you have nothing."

"Okay," I said, standing up. "Well, you'll have to keep me updated."

"On to the Korean War," he said, pumping his hand in the air as if he were leading the charge.

I turned towards the door. "I'll see you later, Mr. Gordon."

"Yes, yes," he said, suddenly polite. He stood up to see me out. He could be very gracious, almost gentlemanly, when he wasn't talking about war or politics or social context. In everyday life, he would suddenly become considerate and charming, only interested in making you comfortable. But when he spoke about ideas, his passion overtook his graciousness. I was pretty sure that was what had kept him going almost one hundred years.

"How have you been feeling?" I asked as he walked me to the door, his cane tapping next to him.

"Oh, you know," he said, putting his hand on his hip. "I have some aches and pains, but nothing to complain about."

"My memory's still good," he added, tapping his head. It was clear that was what was most important to him.

I smiled. "Well, keep up the writing, and I'll talk to you later."

He patted me on the shoulder.

"See you next time, kiddo."

Chapter Four

I headed towards Maggie's room with a feeling of dread. I hadn't seen her since our initial meeting, and I felt I should stop by again. I needed to establish the fact that I could deal with her illness and do my job. I was pretty sure I hadn't given her that impression the first time I met her.

When I walked into her room, an older woman who looked to be maybe in her sixties was standing on a chair hanging a poster of a man I didn't recognize. Maggie was directing her from her wheelchair.

"I think you need to go about a hundredth of an inch higher on the left," Maggie was saying.

"Oh, Maggie, stop it," the woman protested. "You know how tired my arms are getting. Now is it straight enough or not?"

"Okay," Maggie laughed. "That's good enough. Even a crooked poster of John Lennon will cheer this place up."

So that's who it was. I cocked my head a little to get a better look. I didn't see it. The black and white poster showed an unsmiling, almost defiant close-up of John Lennon in a dark hat. The "cheeriness" wasn't striking me.

Maggie noticed me then.

"Nora," she exclaimed. I was startled by her enthusiasm. "Come on in and meet my mother."

Maggie's mother climbed down from the chair and brushed herself off. She was wearing jeans and a big man's shirt, and she looked a little dusty and tired, as if this were moving day and she'd had about enough.

She came over and shook my hand. I could see the resemblance to Maggie as she smiled at me. She had gray hair and a deeply lined face that actually didn't look all that much older than Maggie's, and she had the same laughing dark eyes that seemed to always be letting you in on the inside joke, even when you weren't quite sure what it was.

"Hello," she said as she pumped my hand with determination. "You must be the activity director Maggie was telling me about."

"Social worker," I said with some resignation.

"Oh, I'm sorry," her mother said. "She did say social worker. We also did meet the activity director, who I think was a much older woman." She looked back at Maggie for confirmation, but Maggie shook her head.

"The physical therapist."

"Right," her mother continued as if that was exactly what she meant. "Anyway, Maggie was telling me how fresh and young you were and how happy she was to have someone like you here."

"Really?" I said, trying not to sound too surprised. Maybe I hadn't made as bad of an impression as I'd thought.

"So what do you think?" Maggie's mother asked. I looked around the room. There was a smaller photo of several children, probably nieces and nephews, another large poster of a sunset over water, this one truly crooked by more than a hundredth of an inch, a colorful throw on the bed, and a vase with some flowers on the nightstand next to a picture of what looked to be Maggie, her brother and sister, and her parents.

"Very homey," I lied.

"Just what I was thinking," her mother said, winking at me.

"Oh, for God's sake," Maggie said. "Of course it's not homey. I'm not an idiot. At least not yet."

Her mother turned to look at her and for a moment, I thought they might argue. But instead, they both began to laugh.

"Let me know when you are an idiot," her mother said. "Because it sure will make my life a lot easier."

I walked over to look closer at the John Lennon poster.

"I'm a John girl," Maggie told me.

"A John girl?"

"Yeah, you pick your favorite Beatle and that shows what kind of person you are. I'm filled with peace and love and joy," Maggie said, drawing each syllable out in a hippie type voice. She and her mother both laughed.

"Yeah, I'm overwhelmed with your peace and love and joy," her mother said.

"She's a George girl," Maggie said proudly. "A mystic." Maggie seemed awed, as if she really believed it.

I looked from one to the other. I wasn't quite sure what to make of them.

"I think she may be too young to be a Beatles girl," her mother said knowingly.

Maggie nodded. "Go Google them and tell me which one you relate to the most," she told me, as if she were giving me an assignment.

"Okay?" I tried to agree, but it came out as a question.

"Well," her mother said now. "I think I've done as much damage as I can for one day, and I have to get to my yoga class."

She leaned over and kissed Maggie on the top of her head. "You be a good girl," she told her, as if Maggie were a ten-year-old. In some ways, I think Maggie was.

Her mother stuck out her hand to me again. "It was so nice meeting you, Nora," she said.

"You too—" I hesitated. I hadn't gotten any of her names, first or last.

"Diane," she said. "You can call me Diane. I'm sure you'll be seeing me around quite a bit."

I nodded, and with a little wave to Maggie, she was gone.

I simply stood staring for a minute. I had never witnessed a mother-daughter relationship quite like this. They seemed to be friends in one sense, and yet Diane still had that motherly tone with Maggie, even at forty-two. I certainly had never had this kind of relationship with my mother.

"Nora?" Maggie asked. "Is anything wrong?"

"No." I shook myself out of it. "It's just your mother is so different from mine." I paused. "And older," I added. "Yet she seems much younger, yet older at the same time. Do you know what I mean?"

I looked at Maggie. She actually seemed to be following my convoluted thought process.

"My mother's one-of-a-kind," she said, nodding. "I'm very lucky."

I sat down in a chair across from her.

"What is your mother like?" she asked.

I thought about my mother. She had raised me alone after my father left us when I was about six. I'd only seen my father a couple of times after that. He sent cards at first, and I went to his new house for one or two weekends. Maybe it was more than that. I couldn't remember anymore. But he had slowly evaporated from our lives, and then it was just my mother and me. My mother went from man to man, never settling with one for very long, until she finally married her current husband about four years ago. They moved to Florida soon after the wedding, and now I only saw them a couple of times a year.

"I don't know," I said finally. "I don't think I really know my mother."

I thought about how my mother had always been so pretty, even as she aged, how men had always loved her and left her, how she had held jobs in offices, one for almost ten years. She had always resented having to work for a living. Even though my father sent child support sometimes, she felt the burden was all on her and it wasn't supposed to be that way, that a man was supposed to be taking care of her. I thought about how when she married her new husband—my stepfather, I guess he was, though I hardly knew him—that she finally seemed settled, a complete person. Now when I talked to her on the phone, she was light and airy and unconcerned, a Mrs. Somebody. The bitterness was gone, the fear of not making it, the lost soul tone in her voice.

I thought about how all those years that she had struggled to make a living for us and find the right man for herself, I had learned to get along without her. From her dependence, I had learned independence.

"I don't think my mother would come and put posters up for me," I finally said.

"No?" Maggie asked, sounding a little surprised.

"No," I said again, more certain now. "She would do what she had to do, but nothing more. Never anything more."

Maggie looked a little sad, and I suddenly realized it was happening again. Our roles had reversed yet again.

"Oh my God," I said out loud. "I am the worst social worker ever."

"What?" Maggie asked.

"I am supposed to be helping you, not telling you about my mother. You are the one who is sick and needs *my* help." I could hear the panic in my own voice.

"Nora, calm down," Maggie said soothingly. "I'm a big girl. I don't need your help. Not right now, anyway. I'll let you know as soon as I do."

I looked her in the eye, trying to see if she was telling the truth. She seemed to be.

"Okay, well next time I'll—" my voice trailed off. What would I do for her anyway?

"Cheer me up," Maggie suggested.

"Exactly," I agreed. "I'll cheer you up. I'll figure out what kind of Beatles girl I am and we'll—" I tried to think fast. "We'll make a chart or something that shows which one we are."

Maggie laughed. "I'm not sure we need a chart, but well, okay. Sounds like a plan." She held up her twisted fingers as if to seal the deal, and I took them gingerly in my own hand. We shook on it, as best we could.

I turned around to go and walked into her wheeling bed tray. Before I could even be embarrassed, Maggie chuckled with pure delight.

I could only hurry out of the room in shame.

Chapter Five

"It's God's will for me," Alma Buford droned in a nasally, monotone voice. We'd had this same conversation many times, so I pretty much knew the way it went. She complained about the nursing home, her hip pain, her daughter who never came to visit, her son who had married an awful woman, the television station with the poor reception, the woman in the next room who called out in the middle of the night. It was pretty much the same list of complaints each time, give or take a few. Every suggestion I would try to give would be shot down immediately. And it always ended with her concluding that only God knew her suffering, that it was his will for her to sacrifice, and she had to accept it. I felt completely drained by the end of the conversation.

"Mrs. Buford, would you like me to call the minister of your church to come and visit?" I said. So he can listen to you instead of me, I didn't say.

"No, no," she said. "I don't want to bother him. He has more important things to do." She sniffed. I sensed there was a story in that sniff about how he too had failed her in some way. But I was saved by the nurse's aide bringing in Mrs. Buford's lunch.

"So I hear you can't make it down to the lunchroom today, Alma," the aide said, a little annoyed. Then she noticed me. "Oh, I didn't realize you were talking to the activity director."

"Social worker," I said, sighing.

She set the tray down on the table with a slight bang.

"Well, I'll be on my way, Mrs. Buford," I said.

"You can stay through lunch," the aide said, with maybe just the slightest hint of pleading in her voice.

"No, I really should get going. Enjoy your lunch, Mrs. Buford."

I raced to the door as fast as I could without actually running and almost ran smack into the nurse's aide who was also trying to escape.

"Where's my milk?" Mrs. Buford said with indignation. "I always have a glass of milk at lunch."

The aide sighed and turned back, while I was able to sneak out.

Several patients were lined up in their wheelchairs in the hallway, ones who were unable to feed themselves. One of the local volunteers was there helping to mix the pureed food and spoon it out for the patients.

"Open up, here comes the choo choo train," she said in a sing-song voice. I cringed.

I caught the eye of Cathy, one of the nurses at the desk nearby. She shrugged and shook her head, but then seemed to suddenly remember something, and waved me over. She was leaning down to get something out from under the desk.

"I see Maria's back to volunteer," I said as I came up to the desk.

She sighed. "Yeah, I don't know what to say to her. She means well."

"They've lived out their entire lives, longer than any of us," I said. "Do they really need a choo choo train to deliver their food?"

"Let's just hope they tune her out like we all do." She laughed. "Listen, Nora, I've got something for you." She pulled a big stuffed rabbit out of a plastic bag. "I bought this for my dog, Cheney. But he just hates it. And I know you've got that big galoot of a dog and thought he might like it."

I took it from her, and it squeaked as I grabbed it. "Oh, yeah," I said. "Barney Fife will love this. And maybe he will leave the real rabbits alone then."

She handed me the plastic bag, and I put the rabbit back inside.

"Thanks, Cathy," I said as I started to walk back to my office.

"Buzzz, buzzzz . . ." I could hear Maria's voice in the background as I left. I sighed and began rubbing my forehead, as if her voice were in my head, and somehow that would make it go away.

I was annoyed today, there was no denying it. Between Mrs. Buford and Maria, I was ready to call it a day. And it was only lunchtime.

I thought about Mrs. Buford's belief in God as I came into my office, closed the door, sat down, and put my feet up on the desk. I leaned back in my stiff chair that didn't really lean very well. But I could pretend. I pulled my skirt around my knees and hoped that no one would suddenly open the door.

All I need is a cigar, I thought.

Mrs. Buford was one of my toughest cases, I realized. As if I really had cases. As if I could really make a difference in any of these patients' lives at this stage of the game. But her mind was so set on her misery and there seemed no cure for it. Everyone had failed her. All she had was "God's will." And yet, though she would never admit it, even God had failed her. What do you say to someone like that?

I suddenly was remembering back to the period in my life when my mother had become a born-again Christian. Her new boyfriend was a born-again, so as always, my mother became one soon after she started seeing him. She'd insisted I go to church with them, afraid for my soul, though surprisingly not afraid for her own even though she was having premarital sex, something absolutely forbidden by her new church.

I'd been about twelve, and I remembered that I wasn't quite sure during that period whether I wanted to get along with my mother or disagree with everything she said. I was given no choice in attending the service with them, though. I found it to be one of the strangest, most conflicting experiences of my life. Even to this day. The people all greeted me with a warmth and friendliness I'd found nowhere else. They told me I was "meant to be there." They hugged me and brought me to the front of the church where I was given a special seat next to my mother and her boyfriend, who seemed to be someone fairly important in the church.

And then the service started. As the music began playing, people stood and were swaying back and forth with their arms raised in the air. Even my mother, who was someone who never even listened to the radio, who thought it was a waste of her hard-earned money to buy me CDs or even a CD player, was so taken with the music, so *into it*, that she couldn't contain herself and was swaying and moaning. Then the minister began to shout about Jesus and hell, and how if we didn't accept Jesus as our savior, we would burn in hell. There was no other way, he shouted. And for those of us who weren't saved, *now* was the time, not tomorrow, not next week, not after the Armageddon when it would be too late, but *now*. If we didn't want to burn for eternity, we had better come to the altar to be saved now.

I got my butt up there. Whatever he said had scared a lot of people besides me because there was a line of us. We were all in front of the stage. One by one he went to us and placed his hand on our foreheads. I saw people falling over. I couldn't understand it. I didn't know if they were fainting or if he was somehow pushing them, but when he got to me, I understood. When he touched my forehead, I felt an energy go all the way through my body. I was weak for a second, and my knees started to go out from under me, but then I grabbed the rail and was able to recover. I didn't know what he had done to me, but I was saved. And I was so relieved. The fires of hell would have been too much for me. I couldn't even stand it when it was 90° outside.

As I came back to my seat, my mother was crying. This, too, was incredible. The only time I'd ever seen her cry was when we'd watched *Sleepless in Seattle* on the VCR. But now she was sobbing and hugging me. It was a moment with my mother I'd always remember.

But by the next month, she and the boyfriend had broken up. I continued to go to the church for a while. My mother would drop me off on Sunday mornings, but she'd shake her head when I'd try to get her to come in with me.

"It's just too hard, Nora, with Joe there," she'd say. Or was it John? Or Jerry? Well, whatever his name had been. So I would go in by myself and watch others be saved. I would listen to the minister talk about God's will and how if we turned our lives over to God, everything would be as it should be. After all, we were saved.

"God has a plan for you," he would shout. I never did understand why he had to shout everything he said, but he did. Whether he was happy or sad, excited or disappointed, praising God or defying the Devil, all of it was shouted. At first, it was exciting, thrilling, to be a part of such drama. But then after a while, it just started to give me a headache.

And then there was Erin at middle school, that one girl who made my life miserable. I wasn't cool enough, I wasn't pretty enough. Erin left me out of every party, every trip to the mall. First, I prayed for God to change Erin's heart. Then I prayed for God to change my heart. One day, sobbing silently in the stall in the school bathroom, I prayed for God to strike Erin dead at the mall that afternoon when everyone was there without me. It was then that I knew I needed to leave the church.

"You know," I said to my mother that Sunday when she offered to take me to church. "I think it's all a bunch of bullshit."

"Don't talk like that," my mother said, always concerned about appearances, if not exactly the state of my soul. But she sighed then and said, "You know, Nora. I don't think we're church-going people."

I always remembered that. We're not church-going people. Who were the church-going people? Alma Buford? Susan MacDonald, the MS patient who had died a few months ago, still talking about Jesus' love? Frank?

"Oh my God," I said out loud, not because I was praying but because I had come to a sudden realization. My feet came off the desk with a thud. I was going to Frank's church. Just like my mother went to Joe's or John's or Jerry's. What's his name's.

But of course I didn't really believe any of what they were teaching at Frank's church anyway, I told myself. I sighed with relief. That was the difference.

It was my day for complainers. Mrs. Wellington had just been readmitted to the nursing home the other day after having gone home several months ago. She had been here the first time with a broken hip and had not been happy to have to recover in a nursing home. Luckily for all of us, she had been released to go home after only a few months. But now she was back, the other hip broken. And she was up at the front desk announcing loudly that she wanted to leave. I was called to intervene.

"Mrs. Wellington, let me take you back to your room," I told her.

"Oh, you're all the same," she shouted. "Trying to appease me. I will not be appeased!"

The receptionist looked frantic, and I grabbed the back of Mrs. Wellington's wheelchair.

"Let's just take a little walk," I said, pushing her down the hall in the direction of her room.

"You can't hold me hostage here," she said.

"No one is holding you hostage, Mrs. Wellington," I told her. "You're here because you have a broken hip and you can't stay alone."

"Oh, that's what they say, but I think it's my husband," she growled. "That drunk. He always wanted to get me out of the house, and now he's finally managed it."

"Mrs. Wellington, your husband died ten years ago."

I was suddenly aware of the administrator of the nursing home, up ahead to my left. She looked like she was with a couple in their fifties and was taking them in and out of rooms, pointing at pictures, smiling warmly at everyone she passed. This could only be a prospective family looking at the nursing home for one of their parents. This could only be a disaster.

"Mrs. Wellington, let's talk when we get to your room." The irony of someone so *not* well being named Mrs. Wellington struck me as bizarre at that moment.

But she was on a rampage.

"That good-for-nothing loser," she continued, not exactly yelling, but not speaking quietly either. "He would want me here. He was always trying to get rid of me." We were nearing the happy party, and there was nowhere for me to turn off.

"Even from his grave, he would want me in this shit-ass nursing home," she cried just as we reached the prospective family. The couple stopped abruptly and stared at Mrs. Wellington with frozen smiles on their faces. The administrator gave me a horrified look that meant I would hear about this later, but turned with a smiling face to the family and guided them gently on their tour. I thought I heard phrases like "off her medication," "dementia-induced," "leaving for home soon." But it was really hard to hear anything over Mrs. Wellington's rant, as she continued on about her dead husband as if he were still alive.

"He always told me I'd end up alone. He promised it. With his bottle crashing to the floor as he passed out on the couch." On it went, just like this.

"Mrs. Wellington," I said helplessly. "Really, can we just wait until we get to your room?"

"He thought he was so smart," she ranted on, paying no attention to me.

Fortunately, we were almost there. I turned her into the room and parked her by the bed. Then I sat on it facing her.

"He's the reason I'm here," she concluded triumphantly.

"Look," I said, "I know you hate it here, but none of us can do anything about the fact that you have to stay here right now."

I suddenly realized she was crying. Tears were streaming down her face. In all my dealings with Mrs. Wellington, I had never seen her cry. She had ranted and raved and yelled. She had spoken sarcastically and disgustedly and with complete disdain for everyone around her. But never this.

"I'm just so lonely," she said now. I patted her arm.

"I know," I said.

"I loved that son-of-a-bitch, and he never cared. He never wanted to be with me. And now he's gone and I'm alone. And I'm here. He always wanted to get rid of me, and now he finally has."

She wasn't making much sense, but I just let her talk. What could I say? Who wouldn't be lonely in her situation? I handed her some tissue. Surprisingly, Mrs. Wellington had no desire to tell me the rest of her life story. That was all there was to it, I guess. She was lonely. That *was* her life story.

We sat for a while until she was done.

"Will you be okay?" I asked. She nodded. All the anger was gone. All the disdain. She was so docile as I left that I hardly recognized her.

When I pulled into my driveway that night, my neighbor came out. Emma and Lou were the young couple in their thirties who lived in the house where I rented my apartment. They had no kids, but they did have two dogs that might as well have been their kids. Unlike most landlords, they were actually thrilled when I brought Barney Fife home.

Emma came to my car tonight carrying what looked to be a large steak bone on a paper plate.

"Here," she said, handing it to me. "I bought some bones today and cooked them up for the dogs, but Max is not feeling well. I thought Barney might like it."

"Thanks," I said. "He'll love it."

I went upstairs and heard Barney scratching at the door at the sound of my footsteps. I opened the door and proudly presented the steak bone to him. He was so thrilled, he forgot he had to pee. Then I pulled out the plastic bag with the furry rabbit.

"Oh my God," I said suddenly, staring at the bunny and then back at the bone. "Barney, you are prosperous," I said incredulously.

Chapter Six

My best friend Sharon and I were among the maybe ten people listening to Frank's band at the club on Saturday night. I had to admit, if only to myself, that there was a reason so few people had turned out that night to hear his band. They sucked.

But Sharon and I were barely listening anyway. "Could it really be possible that Barney is manifesting prosperity?" I asked her, still not quite believing what had happened.

"Well, I don't know, Nora," she said. "What did the people at your church say?"

"It's really Frank's church."

"Okay, well what did the people at Frank's church say?"

"I don't know. I didn't tell them. It's all so freaky." I took a swig of beer.

Sharon nodded. "I don't know anything about all of that shit, but it does seem weird."

"Did you know that Einstein was the one who convinced the United States to make the atomic bomb?

She stared at me blankly. "What are you talking about?"

"The atomic bomb," I repeated.

In the background Frank's band was wailing away at some kind of mix of Christian rock and '60s folk music, I think. It was hard to tell.

"I thought we were talking about Barney and his prosperity," Sharon said. "What does the atomic bomb have to do with it?"

"I don't know what we're talking about," I said as I motioned to the server for another round of beers.

Frank had finished his most recent song with a flourish on the guitar. And now he was talking in a low, deep voice, his mouth intensely pushing into the mic.

"I want to play a special song now, a little favorite of mine from a guy most of you are probably familiar with—Johnny Cash."

"Johnny Cash!" Sharon and I both said at the same time.

"I would have never pegged him for a Johnny Cash guy," I said, taking a sip from my new beer.

"Oh God, I hope he's not going to sing that prison song," Sharon said.

I couldn't control myself as my beer came spitting out all over the table, and I began to cough and laugh at the same time.

"I'm pretty sure Frank has never been to prison," I cackled, way too loudly. "His idea of hardship is not getting everything he wants exactly when he wants it."

Sharon was quickly wiping the table, trying to clean up my mess, as if she were afraid someone might notice. "How many drinks have you had?" Sharon asked.

"Just a few beers," I said.

"You can't possibly be drunk on that."

"I may have had a shot or two on my way to the bathroom."

"Well, how many was it?"

"Well, how many times have I been to the bathroom?"

"I don't know, three, maybe four times."

"Then I've had three, maybe four shots."

"Oh my God," Sharon said. "It's a good thing I'm driving."

Frank's voice was low and flat as he attempted to make his voice deeper.

"What the hell is he singing?" I asked Sharon.

"I have no idea," she said, watching him. "I think I heard something about a Sugar Daddy."

"This sure doesn't sound like 'Walk the Line,'" I added. "That's got to be the only song he knows."

Frank's mouth was so close to the mic, it was hard to understand him.

"Oh my God, is he singing to me?" I was horrified. He seemed to be singing something about ending up alone, as he looked right at me, but I couldn't be sure. It's always so hard to tell with country music whether you're being complimented or insulted.

"I think he's serenading you," Sharon said incredulously. "Maybe he sees you as his June Carter." She sounded almost serious.

I put my hands up to cover my mouth, but I was laughing so hard, my whole body was shaking.

"Sharon, stop it. He's looking right at me."

Sharon shoved her napkin to the floor. "Pretend like we're trying to find something under the table." We both bent over and moved our arms around as if we were searching diligently for something valuable.

"He's your Sugar Daddy," Sharon told me under the table.

We couldn't stop laughing. I stopped suddenly as I felt the beer coming up in the back of my throat. "Oh shit, I'm going to throw up."

Sharon shoved the napkin from the floor at me and I stuck it over my mouth and sat up slowly. The beer went back down. Mercifully, the song ended.

"Well, that ends our set for the night," Frank was saying. "You've been a great crowd."

"Crowd?" Sharon asked.

"Sharon, stop or I'm going to hit you," I told her. "You know I can't stop laughing when I drink."

"Okay, I'll be good," she said. "But you need to learn how to handle your liquor better."

"I can't believe he was singing that song to me," I said.

"Well, at least he was thinking about you," Sharon said.

I glared at her. "Shouldn't a minimal requirement be that he not sing to me about how I'll end up alone?" I asked.

Sharon and I often talked about "minimal requirements" in relationships. It was something that was so basic in a relationship you couldn't believe you'd missed it when going out with a guy. It was surprising how often we did miss it.

"Well, I don't know if I'd call it minimal," Sharon said. "But it was kind of odd."

"Odd?! That's an understatement."

Frank was suddenly sliding into the chair beside me. "So what did you think?" he asked me. I stared at him, surprisingly speechless.

"It was great," Sharon lied for me. "We kept talking about your unique sound."

"Yeah, we are unique, aren't we?" Frank said proudly, not realizing that I hadn't answered the question as he glowed in the false praise.

"What were you guys doing under the table during our last song? That's our best one, you know," he said, suddenly as offended as he had been complimented a minute ago.

"Well, Sharon lost her ring and we were trying to find it," I told him quickly, before I had a chance to realize that Sharon still had no ring on her finger. Frank noticed too.

"So, you couldn't find it?" he asked. He started to bend over as if he were going to look for it.

"She realized she never had it on," I said, again much too quickly.

Sharon winced. Frank stared at Sharon a minute, I think trying to figure out how you could think you'd lost a ring you were never wearing. Then he stared at me. Did he know I was lying?

"Are you drunk, Nora?" he asked.

"Well—" I started.

"How do you come to hear me sing for the first time and get drunk?" Once again, he was completely insulted. It was really too much work getting through a night without offending him. The sensitive artist and all that.

"I just maybe had one too many," I said. "I was so excited to hear you."

Sharon winced again. She had always told me what a terrible liar I was. Frank smiled, but I knew he didn't believe me.

"So, why don't you come back to my place tonight?" he asked suddenly, changing the subject.

"You know I can't leave Barney."

"Oh, come on, Nora. Does your life have to revolve around that dog?"

"No, it doesn't," I said defensively. "But he does have to go to the bathroom and crap like that."

I stopped suddenly. "Oh, that's good," I said, giggling. "Crap like that. Wasn't that good, Sharon?"

"Yes, Nora, an amazing pun," Sharon said. Even in my altered state, I could tell she was being sarcastic.

"Why don't we go back to Barney's place?" I said to Frank. "I mean my place."

"My place is five minutes from here. It's so much easier. I think you need to be more flexible. We always go to your place."

I glared at him.

Sharon looked pained. "Here, give me your keys," she said to me, holding out her hand.

"Sharon, you drove."

"Your house keys, dude," she said. I knew Sharon was annoyed because she always used dude when she meant idiot. "I'll go pick Barney up and sneak him into my apartment for the night. You can pick him up tomorrow. He'll be fine."

"I don't know," I said. "What if he barks and gets you kicked out?"

"He won't bark," Sharon said. "And I won't get kicked out. I'm the only one in the building who pays my rent."

Frank was glaring at me.

"Oh, alright," I said and handed my keys to Sharon.

She got up in a hurry. "So Frank, it was so good to hear your band. Nora, I'll see you tomorrow."

And then she was gone, leaving me alone with sullen Frank.

"Could she have gotten out of here any faster?" Frank asked, laughing a little bitterly.

"She hates it when she's drunk and I'm not. " I stopped. "I mean—"

"I know what you mean," he said.

"I think I become dislocated when I drink," I told him.

"Dislocated?" he asked. "What are you talking about?"

"No, I mean—what's the word? You know, everything's backwards."

"Dyslexic?" he asked.

"Yes!" I said, amazed. "This is like charades. How did you get that?" I was pretty sure it was the first time he'd ever fully understood anything I'd said.

"I don't know how I got it. I understand your insanity. Come on, let's go."

"Don't you want a beer?" I asked him.

"Nah, I've got something much better at my place."

He dragged me to my feet, and I stumbled into him.

"I can't believe you're drunk," he said, holding onto me as we made our way to his car. He settled me into the front seat. I was feeling nauseous again.

"Would you happen to have a Kleenex?" I asked as innocently as possible.

"Oh no, not in my car," he said. "I just cleaned it." I looked around me inside his little Ford. I guess it was clean, as clean as a ten-year-old car can ever be.

I swallowed hard and the nausea started to go away. "Alright, let's just go."

He got into the driver's side. It was only a short trip to his place, as he said, and I sat with my head leaning back the whole way, hoping I wouldn't throw up in Frank's clean car.

He lived in the artsy area of town, in an old, turn-of-the-century house converted into apartments. You could tell his place was never meant to be an apartment, with all its strange nooks and surprising turns. The kitchen was in an L shape, like it was the combination of what had once been two large closets. The only bathroom was off the kitchen, and was almost bigger than the kitchen. The bedroom and living room looked like they had once been one large room that had been divided in half to make two rooms. But somehow this strange conglomeration of rooms suited Frank. It was as erratic as he seemed to be sometimes.

We came in, and I fell into his bean bag chair. I was pretty sure Frank was the only person in the world who still had a bean bag chair. I couldn't remember anyone ever having one, but he claimed they were once all the rage and considered it part of his "retro" style. I thought it was just weird.

"Do you have any wine?" I asked, knowing he wasn't a beer drinker.

"No," he said, but he pulled out a tin can from his other retro piece of furniture, the wooden hutch with a chipped stain glass door. I was surprised to see him light a joint.

"Oh, wow," I said watching him take a hit and pass it to me. "This might be a scary conglomeration."

"Combination?" he asked.

"God, you're good," I said, feeling the smoke passing through me. We stayed like that for a while, quietly sharing one joint, then another. I could see Frank relaxing. I was feeling much better too. I was pretty sure I'd read somewhere that one of the medicinal uses of marijuana was for nausea.

"It's all so amazing," I said. My brain had felt like it was floating all night, sometimes awash in waves, other times just drifting. But now, with the pot, I felt like it would suddenly take off in flight, soaring off into whole new areas of understanding.

"What is so amazing?" Frank asked. He was lounging on his couch with the bad cushions.

"Like how it's all so connected, you know. How the atomic bomb changed the world forever, and yet it was a horrible tragedy. And yet it was something that had to happen. You know?"

"Huh?" he asked simply.

"It's just all so connected. It's all so wild. Like Barney being prosperous."

"Barney is prosperous?" Frank asked.

"Yeah," I said, like he was an idiot. "I told him he was prosperous. Like twice. And then he got all these bones. But I said I was prosperous like five hundred times and I got nothing."

Frank looked confused, but also like he didn't really care much. I could tell he didn't even want to make the effort to figure it out.

"You know, Nora," he said. "You make everything so hard. It's all as simple as you said. We're all connected."

"If it's all so simple, why are we all so fucked up?"

He sighed. "I don't know about that," he said. "I have to wonder that myself. What the hell is wrong with everyone, anyway?"

We both pondered it quietly for a moment. We didn't have any answers. I don't think we wanted any answers. We just wanted to think about it and pretend we were trying to understand it.

"What would God say about all this deblokery?" I asked suddenly, motioning to the joint and the smoke, as if we were awash in it.

"This what?" asked Frank. He seemed to have lost his ability to interpret.

"What's the word? You know what I'm trying to say."

"Debauchery?"

"Yes!" I exclaimed. "We have to go on one of those game shows." Frank laughed. "What would God say about us doing this?"

"With everything going on in this world right now—the wars, people starving, people dying of Aids, you know, all of it—do you really think God cares that you and I are getting a little high? He's probably saying— take it where you can. Have a little fun."

I think I stared at him in amazement. "Wow, Frank," I said, "you are so cool when you're high."

He smiled. "Yeah, that's what everyone says."

"So maybe you should get high more often."

"Nah, then I'd be a pothead. And you know what they say about potheads."

"What's that?"

"They never go anywhere in life. I want to go somewhere."

He stood up, and took my hand suddenly. "Come on," he said.

I stumbled up and he led me into the bedroom. I fell onto his mattress on the floor, another retro style, I guess—the hippie look. Or just the starving artist look. Frank lowered himself on top of me.

"Does God want us to do this too?"

"Sure," Frank said. "It's all part of the deblokery."

Chapter Seven

"Don't you think liking my dog should be a minimal requirement?" I asked Maggie, who was lying back in bed, her pillows propped under her.

"Yes," she said simply.

"I mean, if it's important to me, shouldn't he at least make an effort?"

"Yes," she agreed.

I looked at her. "Why are you in bed again?" It was at least 11:00 on Monday morning. It seemed Maggie should be up and in her wheelchair by now.

"I just have bad days, Nora," she said in an annoyed voice. "I'm tired."

"Does the physical therapist agree with your being in bed?"

"Not exactly," she said. "But I do have some choice left in life, don't I?"

It was hard to argue with that.

"I'll be back at it tomorrow," she said, smiling. But it was an uneasy smile, one that told me she wasn't quite sure. I knew as a social worker I should say something, do something, accomplish something in this moment. But I just didn't know what it was.

"So you do agree with me?" I asked again, not quite sure I believed her.

"Yes," she said. "I think he should try to like your dog. Or at least accept the fact that your dog is important to you."

I sat down in the chair next to the bed, thinking this over.

"Well, my friend Sharon keeps telling me I'm making too much of it. She thinks I'm too picky, and I expect too much, and all of that. I don't get it. I mean, we're always talking about how we'll end up sharing a room at the county nursing home—"

Maggie laughed. "The county nursing home? You can do better than that."

"Not on my salary. But she's always talking about how we'll be there for each other when no one else is, but then every guy that comes along, she's pushing me at him. I don't get it."

"I don't know," Maggie said, sighing. "Sometimes friendships can be as hard as relationships, can't they?"

"You think?" I asked.

She sighed again. "I don't know what happened to most of my girlfriends," she said. "I got married and I had my career, and then I got sick. It just seemed like I was always so busy. You know, they tried to be helpful, but they just didn't understand." She paused. "I guess I just let most of those friendships fall by the wayside."

She was quiet now as she considered it all. I wasn't sure what to say, so I said nothing.

"It was hard to keep up the charade," Maggie continued, deep in thought. "They wanted to get together for lunch and talk about their kids or the latest divorce, that kind of thing. When I first got sick, I felt like I just lived in a state of terror about what was going to happen to me. It was hard to talk about someone's new hairstyle when I felt like that, you know?"

"That must have been awful," I said, feeling like I had just been doing the same thing—talking about my superficial life when she was struggling just to get out of bed.

"Well, as I went along and my symptoms weren't that bad," she continued, as if to comfort me, "I was less terrified and it was more like I just had this nagging fear, and I knew if I stopped long enough to listen to it, that it would blow back up again into something I couldn't handle. So I stayed busy as much as I could, trying to ignore it. But it was always there, in the back of my mind."

"I'm sorry," I said. "I just came in here and did the same thing. Talking about some guy I'm not even sure I like that much when you're having a hard time."

"No, no," she said, reaching out her crooked hand to pat my arm as best she could. "I didn't mean that. I don't mind hearing about him. It's important for you to figure out if he's right for you. I'm just doing a lot of thinking out loud right now. Don't mind me."

"It seems like a lot of times with friends that all we end up talking about is men."

Maggie nodded. "I've noticed that too."

"Doesn't it seem like we should have something else to talk about?"

Maggie laughed. "Well, you know, the biological urge and all that."

"Oh God," I said. "Is that all it is?"

Maggie laughed again. "Oh, Nora, you crack me up," was all she said.

"I mean, isn't there anything more than that in life?"

"Let's hope so," she said. "Because it looks like I'm about done with mine."

Once again, I felt like I had taken us to a place in the conversation I hadn't really meant to. It was so hard not to end up reminding her of her losses. Was that how her friends had felt too?

"There were so many times when I wanted to tell people how afraid I was," she said quietly. "I wanted to tell them how hard it was, but I don't know, it just never felt like I could. It felt like they wanted me to be okay with it all, to be dealing with it in a positive way, and so I tried to pretend that I was. But it was so hard to pretend. I guess I just kind of gave up."

"Well, do you want to talk about it now?" I asked.

Maggie smiled, somewhat sadly. "You know what's strange? I'm not as afraid as I was. I think the anticipation of what would happen was so much worse. Now that I'm actually—well, what am I? I guess I'm disabled, aren't I?" She shook her head slightly as if she couldn't believe it. "It's so hard to think of myself that way, but that's what I am now, isn't it? But it was the fear of what would happen or could happen that drove me crazy. Now that it's actually happened, it's not as frightening. It's just so strange." She chuckled to herself. "I was terrified of ending up in a nursing home. That was one of my worst fears. And here I am."

Maggie had been lost in her own thoughts, not looking at me as she confessed her fears, but now she turned and saw my expression. I didn't want to tell her how disturbed I was by what she was saying, but she must have seen it on my face.

"Nora, really, it's not as bad as you might think," she said.

"To hear you talk about how afraid you were of being in a nursing home, and then here you are, it's just—" I didn't know how to finish my sentence.

"It's just terrifying to think that your worst fears can come true, isn't it?"

"Yes," I said. "That's it."

"But see that's what I'm saying. The fear of it is so much worse than the reality." She held up her arm and swept it slowly around the room. "Not that this is where I want to be, of course, but it's not the horror I thought it would be. It's just another step in a life I wasn't expecting to lead."

I could only stare at her, taking it all in.

"You know I think what makes anything so hard—whether it's getting MS or something else, anything that you have to deal with in life—what makes it so hard is doing it alone. It's feeling like you have all this fear and craziness inside, but there's no one who can really understand it. Do you know what I mean?"

"Yes," I said, nodding.

"And yet, maybe there is no other way we can really do it, but alone. Because in the end, who can really understand what you're going through? I'm not sure anyone can. Even someone else with the same disease or the same problem. Do they really know what it's like for you? Aren't we all just inside our own worlds?"

She looked at me like she expected answers, but I knew by now that Maggie wasn't expecting any answers from me. It was such a relief.

We were both silent for a minute, not sure what to say.

"So does all of this mean I should dump Frank?" I asked finally, hoping to lighten the mood. Or maybe I really thought we'd still been talking about men all this time.

Maggie laughed. "I think you should listen to yourself and not me or anyone else," was all she said.

We were silent again.

"Did you figure out what kind of Beatles girl you are?" she asked finally.

"Yes," I said, eager to move on. "I'm a Paul girl."

"No, you're not."

"What?"

"You're not a Paul girl. Go back and look again."

"I don't need to look again. I'm a Paul girl," I said. I felt like I was flunking a test I hadn't even known I was taking.

"Try again," she said simply.

"But you just told me to listen to myself and not to you or anyone else," I protested.

"Yes, but you're not listening to yourself if you think you're a Paul girl."

"Why can't I be a Paul girl? I think he's cute."

"Yes, he's cute, but you're not a Paul girl. Those are the outgoing, happy types. That's not you."

I sighed. "This is crazy. Okay, I'll try again."

Maggie smiled. "Of course you will." I left her that way, smiling and satisfied with herself, still deep in thought.

I went back to my office, closed the door and sat at my desk. I had piles of paperwork to do, but I just sat staring at my potted plant. I couldn't bring myself to do anything. I found myself thinking about my friend Myra from high school, and how she had gotten me involved in a project for the homeless at a local church. It was probably my first real experience with social work, the time when the seed had been planted. And it was at a church.

What is it with me and churches? I wondered. It was like I was always hanging around these churches, but never really joining any of them. It was like I was always hanging around God, but never really getting him.

So Myra asked me if I wanted to help her out during the month before Christmas. Every Friday after school we drove down to this church in the city where they had a food window for homeless people. Myra and I collected boxes of food from the local grocery store to take down there.

I remember that's what I liked most about my friend Myra. She was always involved in some kind of project and was way too busy to be worried about boys and how she looked. She always wore the same thing—jeans, a collared shirt, and clogs or boots. My other friends used to mock her out behind her back, making fun of her different colored shirts. If she wore a new one, they noticed and pointed it out to each other. I would laugh along with the joke, but I secretly admired her ability not to care what people thought. I'd lost touch with her after high school and never knew for sure what happened to her. It seems like I'd heard that she'd gone on to be a missionary somewhere in South America, or maybe she'd joined the Peace Corps? Something very cool like that.

But I hated Christmas back then. I still do, I guess. Every year it was the same. My mother and I would go to my grandparents' house and sit around uncomfortably, talking about nothing. We'd eat the same thing every year—ham with scalloped potatoes. In my mother's family, this meal was a Christmas tradition of unknown origin, but one that had to be followed every year. After dinner, we'd all open gifts and exclaim over the scarves and socks we'd never expected to receive.

But that month I spent bringing food to the church with Myra was one of the best Christmas seasons I could ever remember. We would drive down to the church in her mother's van and unload all the boxes. Sammy, the housekeeper and cook, would always meet us at the van. She was a tiny woman, who couldn't have been more than five feet tall, and so thin she looked like she couldn't lift a box of tissue, but she'd carry one heavy box after another inside.

After we'd unload the van, Sammy would have us sit at the table and she'd make hot chocolate for us. She always had cookies or brownies too, just to make sure we had as big of a sugar high as we could get. To me, the kitchen always smelled of roast beef and mashed potatoes. Sometimes Sammy would have us taste whatever she was cooking, never roast beef and mashed potatoes, more like chicken casserole, and once I think it was a rather spicy spaghetti sauce. I never smelled any of that, though, just the roast beef and mashed potatoes.

Sammy was old, in her seventies at least, but she had so much energy. She would sing as she cooked. It was always some old song that sounded vaguely familiar, but we weren't really sure what it was. Myra and I would exchange smiles at how tone deaf she was, but we never let on. I had a feeling no one had ever let on and poor Sammy thought she was entertaining everyone with her lovely voice.

That year my mother actually had a fiancée. As we sat at the table one Friday drinking our hot chocolate, I was telling Myra about how we were going to be spending Christmas with my mother's boyfriend's family. I was nervous about it, about Christmas at a stranger's house, but even more so, about the wedding and having a new stepfather and being forced into a whole new life I wasn't sure I wanted. I was trying to pretend it all didn't matter to me, putting on an air of nonchalance that Myra seemed to accept. Sammy was stirring something in a huge pot on the stove, and I didn't even think she was listening to our chatter, but suddenly she came over and put her hands on my shoulders.

"Whatever will be, will be, honey," she said simply and squeezed my shoulders. I had to look down so that Myra wouldn't see the tears in my eyes. Sammy had heard all of my unspoken terror at what was happening. Everyone else in my life had bought my bravado, but somehow Sammy had not.

That Christmas with the boyfriend's family actually made me long for my grandparents' house. We went to his mother's house where there seemed to be hundreds of aunts and uncles and cousins. In reality, there were probably only about forty people. For reasons I never fully understood, everyone kept thinking my name was Dora. I suspect it was my mother's boyfriend who was never sure what my name really was, and so had told his whole family the wrong thing, but my mother would never admit to that and refused to let me tell the story that way. By the end of the evening, her boyfriend's uncle, who was very drunk on the eggnog, kept putting his arm around me and announcing, "Here is Dora the Explorer." It was beyond embarrassing for a seventeen-year-old, not to mention that there was something a little creepy about the way he said "explorer." All I could picture was spending the rest of my life coming to Christmas dinner at this awful place, forever being known as "Dora the Explorer."

Thankfully, the wedding was off by February and my mother went on to marry her current husband after I had gone to college. It was something I would always be grateful for. He has a very nice, small family that I never see.

I thought of Sammy now and how warm her kitchen was, with the wonderful smells and the sounds of her banging pans. Even her awful singing voice was welcoming. It was all so different from my family and the Christmas at the boyfriend's house. Somehow this old woman I hardly knew had been able to hear me in a way no one else in my life could, and I didn't know why. Like Maggie, I didn't understand why it was so hard to tell people what I really felt and why it seemed so hard for them to hear it.

I thought of Myra and how she had wanted more out of life than nice clothes and a cute boyfriend. Even in high school, she knew she was destined for something so much more important. Why did she know that? Why didn't I know that about myself?

I suddenly sat back in my seat with a start. The inflexible office chair sounded like it might crack in half, but I ignored it. I realized now why I had become a social worker. Not because I wanted to help other people, not because I had something to offer those who had less than me, but because I wanted to find something for myself. I wanted be destined for something more important, like Myra was. But even more, I realized now as I sat in my tiny office with a dying plant and a stack of paperwork on dying patients, I wanted to smell the roast beef and mashed potatoes of Sammy's warm kitchen.

Chapter Eight

I was sitting next to Frank in church that Sunday watching as one by one each person moved forward in line and added the flame from his or her small candle to the larger candle in the front. There was soft music playing, and everyone was silent, perhaps in meditation? I couldn't be sure.

"So this represents oneness?" I whispered to Frank. We'd arrived too late to get our own candles and had missed the minister's explanation.

He shrugged. "Probably," he whispered back, with a total lack of passion.

I was annoyed. "Well, Frank, if you don't know, how am I supposed to know?" I whispered more fervently. "How am I supposed to understand this spiritual stuff?"

Frank was obviously just as annoyed. "Well, Nora, maybe I'm not responsible for your spiritual enlightenment," he whispered back loudly. Two people in the row in front of us turned to stare. I sat back in my seat and stifled my answer back to him. He probably had a point.

The candle ceremony was coming to an end and the woman minister stood back up at the podium. I still could not get used to having a woman as a minister, even in this day and age. And I kept expecting her to shout at us, or at least to warn us loudly about hell and the evils of the world. But she did none of that. She always talked in a quiet, soothing voice. She told us how loved we were by the universe— not necessarily by God, I noted—but by the universe at large. This confused me. How could a universe love you?

"Thank you," she said now as people settled back into their seats and a rustling seemed to overtake the audience. "Thank you for indulging me in my need to connect, to remember how we are all one."

She paused and gave the audience a big smile as she looked around, taking us all in. "But I want us to consider it in on an even larger scale today. What would it mean to the world if we all knew we were one? If I hurt you and I knew I was really only hurting myself? If I took from you and I knew I was really only taking from myself? How would that make the world different?"

Frank leaned forward, as if he were very interested in this concept.

"Better yet, what would the world look like if we really knew we created our own reality? Oh, I know we talk about it a lot here on Sundays and in our meetings. But how much do we really know that and practice it?"

I thought of Mrs. Avery, lying helpless in her bed at the nursing home, surrounded by tubes. Was this a reality she had created? I thought of Maggie, slowly losing the functioning of her body. I thought of the people who worked at the nursing home, like me, who went into this building day after day to deal with old, sick and dying people. Was this a reality that all of us somehow wanted?

"We have to look at the world we've created," the minister was saying, "and understand how we can create a better reality. How all of us, as part of the oneness, can create the world we truly want. As we do that, as we truly create as loving beings of the universe, then it spreads. I affect you, you affect me. It all comes together."

That's it? I thought. That's the answer—we can create the world we really want? We can go from a world of suffering and pain to a world of love and peace just like that? I tried to picture Maggie rising from her wheelchair, suddenly healed, or Mrs. Avery knocking the tubes away from her bed and standing up, or any of them—Mrs. Wellington suddenly happy with her life, or the nurse's aides waking up to a paycheck that actually rewarded them for the hard work they did. Could it be that easy?

"I've asked some special people to share today," the minister was saying. "They all have stories about creating their reality that I want you to hear."

And one by one, they stood up, sharing their "testimonials," you could almost call them. John, who created a business out of nothing after losing his job. Stan, who had cancer and prayed for healing. Melanie, who found the relationship she'd always wanted by making a list of the qualities she wanted in a man. I glanced over at Frank. You had to be careful with that one, I thought. Frank had most of the qualities I thought I wanted in a boyfriend, and yet—somehow he annoyed the hell out of me.

On they went through a few more stories. I was growing bored. They were all the same. Misery followed by complete happiness. If it were that easy, I thought, why aren't we all doing it?

At one point, Frank reached over and touched my hands that were folded in my lap. I looked over at him. He's getting romantic now? I thought. But I realized I'd been cracking my knuckles. I stopped and he smiled patiently.

Finally, the service came to an end and we moved into the adjoining room for social hour.

"Wonderful service," Frank murmured in my ear as he followed me.

"Yes," I tried to agree.

"Oh, Nora, you were bored out of your mind. You always crack your knuckles when you're bored."

"You don't know that about me," I said indignantly, completely offended that he was so right.

"I know everything about you," he joked.

"You wish," I said.

"I'll go get us some coffee," Frank said. Before I could stop him, he was walking over to the line without me. I knew he was having caffeine withdrawal since we had been running so late and had no time for coffee, but now I had a dilemma on my hands. I could follow him to the line and admit that I was uncomfortable being by myself in the midst of all this "oneness," or I could try to talk to someone I didn't know and pretend I understood all of these concepts that I really didn't get at all, or I could go to the literature table and rifle through all the pamphlets and books, waiting for Frank to come find me and give me a hard time for not mingling with all the oneness around me. As I stood there helplessly, weighing my impossible options, I heard a voice behind me.

"Hello, I don't believe we've met." I turned around to find myself face to face with the minister of the church. I was suddenly nervous, as if I were meeting a celebrity.

"I'm Nora Sullivan," I said, reaching out to shake her hand.

"Rev. Fee," she said warmly, as she shook my hand enthusiastically.

"I don't believe I've seen you here before," she said.

"Well, I have been coming for a few weeks now, maybe more than a month," I said, trying to remember how long it had been. "Well, not every week," I added guiltily.

She smiled. "We don't count here. You're welcome to come as often as you like and you don't receive demerits for not attending. We're trying to get away from the fire and brimstone model of Christianity." She chuckled at that.

"Yes, I've noticed," I told her. "It's still something I expect in church, I guess, but it's a nice change."

"The universe is a loving place," she said confidently. I didn't think I could share that confidence, but I admired it in her.

"I guess that's one thing I wonder about," I said, feeling more comfortable suddenly, my need to understand greater than my nervousness at speaking to the most important person in the room. "You talk so often about the universe. Why is that? How is that different from God or some kind of higher power?"

"Well, it's not different really," she said. "The universe is just what we're all a part of, what we're all made up of. So often when we speak of God, we picture a person, and really, can God be a person? Is he some old man in the sky with a white beard looking down on us? I think not. So we talk of the universe as a way of understanding where creation really comes from, not from a man, or even a woman, but from the fabric of reality."

I wasn't sure I had any idea what she was talking about. But I continued anyway.

"So it's sort of like you ask the universe for what you want and you get it?"

"Sort of," she said, smiling. "We create our reality all the time with our thoughts. It's a matter of training those thoughts to create what you really want—something positive rather than negative."

"But say your reality is overwhelmingly negative. Say you're sick and dying, or in the middle of a war, for example. It's as simple as changing your thoughts?"

Before she had a chance to answer, I heard Frank's voice behind me. "Nora, are you bombarding Rev. Fee with your questions?" I could hear the embarrassment in his voice, the fear that I was somehow making him look bad, without him even knowing what I was saying. It annoyed me.

"Nora has some rather intense questions," Rev. Fee admitted. I didn't think they were so intense. They seemed rather obvious to me. "But I'm sure you can straighten her out, Frank."

Frank handed me my cup of coffee and started to guide me away from her as if I were a child. "I'll give you a rest," he said to Rev. Fee. She seemed relieved to be moving on.

I waited until we were out of earshot. "Do you have to make it seem like I'm some kind of heretic who has come to burn down the church? I was just asking a few questions."

"Don't be so dramatic," he told me. "I didn't act like that. But you can be intense, you know."

"Why? Because I don't accept everything at face value? Because I don't walk out of the service saying it was wonderful every week without having any idea what they're really talking about?"

"I know exactly what they're talking about," he said, not defensively enough, if you ask me. "I don't accept everything at face value. But I don't feel the need to question every detail either."

"You don't question anything, Frank," I said in a disgusted tone. "You just repeat platitudes that don't really mean anything."

"I don't know why you're so angry about everything, Nora."

"I'm not angry about everything. I'm angry that you want everything so nice all the time, when it's just not. And then you say that that's being spiritual."

"What do you know about spirituality?" he challenged.

"Nothing," I admitted. There was silence. He didn't know what to do with that.

"Let's just go," he said.

It wasn't soon enough for me.

Chapter Nine

"I am not talking to a seventy-year old man about sex," I told Allison, one of the nurses at Longate. She was the only nurse there who was my age and we would often have conversations about different bars or concerts we'd been to. But now she had cornered me in the nurse's station and told me I needed to have a talk with Mr. Halloran about his inappropriate behavior.

"Who else is going to do it? You're the social worker."

"So it's my job to do what no one else wants to?"

"Pretty much," she laughed. I sighed.

"Well, Nora," she continued. "This is a social problem, after all. We can't have him pinching women's butts and making these kinds of remarks. Not only is it embarrassing, but it could get the nursing home in trouble."

"No one is going to sue over an old man with dementia," I told her.

"Oh, come on," she said. "You can sue because your coffee is too hot."

I sighed again.

Allison's voice got lower. "None of these older nurses are going to deal with this," she said conspiratorially, appealing to this vague sense of camaraderie we shared. We were in this together, the young ones taking control in this strange world of the old and dying, or something along those lines. I felt it whenever we talked, though we'd never specifically put it into words.

"Okay," I finally agreed. "I can't believe I have to do this."

I started to walk away from the nurse's station.

"Make sure you document it in his chart," Allison called out behind me.

I didn't turn around but raised my hand in acknowledgement. "Yeah, and I'll wrap it in plain brown paper," I called back. I could hear Allison laughing behind me.

I found Mr. Halloran in a common room where patients were watching TV. He was dozing when I tapped on his wheelchair and I watched as his head shook slightly and his eyelids fluttered open and shut for a full minute, as if they might never open fully again. But then finally he looked up at me, a little groggily.

"Mr. Halloran, I need to talk to you in my office," I told him crisply.

"I'll go anywhere with you, baby," he said, as I went behind his wheelchair and began pushing it down the hallway as gruffly as I could. He seemed completely undisturbed by my manner.

I maneuvered the chair into my office, closed the door, and sat across from him at my desk.

"Mr. Halloran, we need to talk," I said, still trying to chastise him, but he didn't seem to notice.

"You have nice legs," was his answer.

"I have pants on today," I told him, but didn't mention that besides that fact, my legs were behind the desk. He peaked around to get a look.

"You have beautiful ankles," was his conclusion.

"Mr. Halloran, no one has beautiful ankles," I said. Again, he seemed unaffected by this piece of information and continued to stare lustily at my ankles.

I moved them farther under the desk.

"Mr. Halloran," I continued in the most official voice I could muster under the circumstances, "it has been brought to my attention that you are making inappropriate remarks and gestures to some of the women guests who come to visit other patients here."

He looked confused. I could see the wheels spinning—what exactly did I mean by inappropriate? What did I mean that it had been brought to my attention when it was obvious he made all of the same remarks and gestures to me? Was this some kind of joke or should he take it seriously?

Finally, he brushed his hand in front of this face and said, "Ahh, they love it."

"What exactly do they love?" I asked him, already beginning to lose my professionalism.

"They love the attention. I make them feel wanted."

I was genuinely confused. "Seriously?" I asked. "You seriously think that?"

"Of course," he said. "Women love to have attention from men. Always have, always will."

I sat back in my chair. How could I approach this? Attention from men—maybe. Attention from a seventy-year old man in a wheelchair with drool coming out of his mouth—not really.

"Mr. Halloran, it seems to make many of the women who come here uncomfortable," I said. "This is not a singles bar. They're not coming here to get attention from men. They are coming here to visit family members who are sick and—" I paused. "Who are sick," I said again.

"Yeah, and I help cheer them up," he said. "I make their day."

I sighed. I had been worried about the embarrassment of it all, the discomfort in talking about this with him. I hadn't expected a debate about what women really want.

"Mr. Halloran," I said, again trying an official tone of voice. "You can't act like that towards the women guests, or towards the nurses for that matter, or towards me. It's not appropriate."

"Ahh," he said again, once more waving his hand in front of his face as if he were waving it all away. "You all love it."

"Okay, look," I said, dropping the professionalism. "Women do not love it. We do not enjoy being harassed with sexual remarks and poked at and having our butts pinched. That is not what women want from you."

"Of course you do," he said simply.

"Why do you think that?"

"Let me tell you somethin'," he said. "In my younger days, I was quite a fellow. Maybe not so much any more," he admitted with some reluctance, "but in my day, I was somethin' else. And the women, they all wanted a piece of me."

I wasn't sure what to say. "So you think they still do?" I asked finally.

He hesitated. "You know, I used to go to the bar every night after work. I worked in construction, you know?" I nodded. How could I not know? Even if it hadn't been in his social history, it wouldn't have been a stretch to figure that one out. "The women used to drape themselves all over me. I didn't have to do nothin' to get their attention. The guys always used to say, 'Hey Halloran, when are you gonna settle down?'" He shook his head with a certain cockiness. "Never did. Never had to. I could get myself a different woman every night." He finished the story with a sense of victory in his voice.

"So you never married?" I asked, even though I already knew the answer.

"Never had to," he repeated.

"Well, Mr. Halloran," I said, fumbling around for something to say to make him understand. "As I mentioned, this isn't a bar. The women here are not like the women you met in the bars when you were younger."

"Yeah, they ain't comin' to see me," he agreed. "But I make them wish they had." There was just the slightest sadness in his voice. "Nobody's comin' to see me these days, I guess. Not like the old days."

"Do you wish someone was coming to see you?"

"Nahh," he said, again waving his hand in front of his face. "I had my fun. Those were the days, huh?" He said it like I was one of his old buddies, someone who could remember with him.

"Yeah, those must have been good days," I agreed.

"Drinkin' and smokin' and the women. Geez, never mind the women. These days you can't even have a good smoke without the whole world getting' on your case." I didn't even want to consider if he was trying to smoke in his room. That would have to wait for another conversation.

"You know, I just want to have some fun. What's wrong with you broads that you don't want to have some fun?"

"Well, it's a very different situation."

"Ahh," he said. "Not so different. You all love it." This was obviously his mantra.

"Did you keep in touch with any of your old buddies?" I asked.

"Nah, they had their families, their lives. After I got out of construction, I fell off the roof and broke my back, you know?" I didn't know. Somehow this major detail of his life had never been mentioned. "The guys came to see me in the hospital, but then there was the reha-biliation," he drew out the word to say it correctly, but stumbled over it anyway, "and Uncle Sam paid for my apartment, you know, and then I was here. The guys forgot me after a while. But I had my fun," he said again, as if convincing himself. "Those were the days, huh?"

"Yes," I said. "Those were the days." There seemed to be nothing left to say.

He sat silently for a minute, contemplating "those days."

"I had my fun," he said again, with some reservation this time.

"So Mr. Halloran, do you think you can act more appropriately towards the women here? No more sexual remarks, no more pinching?"

"Ahh," he said, waving his hand in front of his face. "They love it."

I sighed and stood up. "Well, this has been a productive conversation."

"Any time you want to talk, baby, you just let me know. Any time."

I pushed his wheelchair out the door.

"You'll wear a skirt tomorrow, huh?"

"Probably not," I said. "Probably never again."

"Ahh, you will."

I pushed Mr. Halloran back to the common room. If it came to a lawsuit, I had done what I could. Which was obviously nothing.

Chapter Ten

I hit the snooze button for the third time and groaned when I saw the clock. Then I rolled over right onto Frank.

"Oh shit!" I said.

"Good morning to you too," he mumbled.

"I forgot you were here and I'm late again." I fell onto my back, not getting up anyway. What was the point? I'd still be late even if I jumped out of bed and hurried.

"Well, what are they going to do, fire me?" I asked no one in particular. "What other sucker would they find to do this job?"

Frank mumbled something into his pillow and then rolled over onto his back too.

"What?" I said.

"I'm sure there are plenty of people who would do your job."

"What people?" I asked. "I don't even want to be there most of the time."

"You're helping people," he said with sleepiness in his voice. "You must be so selfish to not like a job where you're helping people."

I sat up. "What did you just call me?"

Frank's eyes flew open. I could tell he'd been speaking truths in his half-sleep state and only now realized what he'd said.

"I just meant that it should feel good to help people."

"Frank, what do you even know about this? What do you know about helping people? You're a fucking musician. What do you know about what I do every day?"

"Oh, Nora, calm down," he said, now fully awake. That was good because he was about to be out on the street.

"I don't want to calm down. Just get out of here."

"Do we have to start the day like this?"

"Yes, we do," I said, getting up and grabbing my robe. "Because you just insulted me. Because you think it's okay to tell me what I'm supposed to feel about something you know nothing about."

He started to get up and gather his clothes as I went into the bathroom.

"I can't believe you're being like this," he was saying. "I mean, it's a job. You let it get to you too much. Maybe if you went in there with a positive attitude, you could actually make a difference. Maybe you could actually help them instead of always being so angry and depressed yourself."

I opened the bathroom door. Barney Fife was standing outside it, looking at me sheepishly. "Come on, Barney," I said and he scampered in. "Don't let the screen door hit you on the way out," I called to Frank as I slammed the door closed again.

"Like this dump would have a screen door," he called back.

I opened the bathroom door again. "Yeah, who lives in a dump?"

"Your coffee sucks anyway." The door slammed behind him, but unfortunately, I don't think it hit him.

He was right about one thing. It was a bad way to start the day.

When I got to work, I immediately got a call from the nurse in Maggie's area.

"Nora, oh good, you're here," she said. I could tell from the tone of her voice she'd been trying to reach me and was annoyed I was late.

"What's wrong?" I asked.

"I'm hoping you can talk to Maggie. She's refusing to get out of bed." I thought about the last time I stopped in to see Maggie and she'd been in bed then. That was days ago. The nurse was continuing, "The physical therapist is concerned. We're all concerned. I know you've developed kind of a rapport with her and we're hoping you can talk to her, maybe encourage her to get up and around again."

"I'll be right down," I told her.

When I got to the nurse's station, the nurse continued to fill me in. "The physical therapist feels she can still make strides, still keep pushing herself. She'll never be back to her old self, of course, but it's too early for her to give up. We want her to maintain her quality of life."

"Has she talked to you about why she's not getting up?" I asked. "Maybe she's in pain."

The nurse shook her head. "Not any more than usual," she said. "Her mother has been in to see her every day, but she's had no more luck than any of us. She just seems depressed. It's doubtful she'll respond to you either, but I figured it wouldn't hurt to try."

"Okay," I told her. "I'll give it a try."

I walked to Maggie's room, not sure what I was going to say to her. I knocked gingerly and heard her call out for me to come in. She was lying back on the pillow, the TV blaring some kind of talk show.

"Hey, Maggie," I said hesitantly. "How are you?"

She looked at me. She seemed to be the same old Maggie. "I'm okay," she said. "How about you?"

I shrugged. For once, I thought we should have a conversation about her.

"The nurse tells me you're not getting up," I said as I came closer to the bed. She sighed and turned back towards the TV.

"Oh dear," she said. "So they called you about this. They've decided to bring in the big guns."

I laughed, a little tentatively. "So what's going on?"

"Nothing's going on," she said in an irritated voice. "I have a disease, remember? It's called Multiple Sclerosis. It's debilitating and sometimes life threatening. That's what going on."

"But the physical therapist says you can still—"

"Oh, fuck the physical therapist," she said suddenly with such force that I took a step backwards. "The physical therapist doesn't know anything. She just wants to pat herself on the back at the end of the day and tell herself how much she's done for me. She's not doing jack shit for me. This disease is incurable. Did anyone tell you people that?"

I was speechless. I had never seen her like this. She was like a different person.

"Maggie," I stuttered, "this is not you. You know how to deal with all of this better than anyone I know."

"Nora," she said, turning to me with such fury that I took yet another step back. "I know you want me to be your hero, but I can't be that for you. Do you hear me? You want someone to make it all better for you, someone with a horrible disease who is still wonderful and kind and loving and inspires the world. I am not that person!"

By now she was almost yelling.

"Maggie, I don't—"

"Just get the hell out of here," she finally did yell. I started to back out of the room and then turned to go and almost ran straight into the nurse who was coming in the door.

"What in the world?" she asked.

"I don't think I'm helping," I said in what could be the biggest understatement ever.

She patted my arm. She was an older nurse with a motherly air about her. "Don't take it personally, honey," she said. "She yelled at the physical therapist too. You did your best."

I nodded but couldn't say anything. I just walked slowly back to my office. I went in and closed the door and sank into my chair. I was shaking.

I couldn't believe the change in Maggie in such a short time. I couldn't believe she had just kicked me out of her room. But I knew immediately what was happening—"Instant Karma." I had furiously kicked Frank out of my apartment this morning and now Maggie had just done the same to me. It was inevitable. The only reason I even knew anything about this was because Maggie had me researching the Beatles to find out what kind of Beatles girl I might be. I had come across the song by John Lennon and had been intrigued by it. Now it was happening to me.

I just kept sitting at my desk, trying to stop shaking. What could I do? How could I help her? I knew that she was right about all of it. We were all acting like nothing was wrong, that with enough physical therapy, one day she'd get up and walk again. I knew that it must be impossible to be in a nursing home at the age of forty-two, knowing that this was the rest of your life, however long or short it might be, and the only person who came to see you was your mother. And most of all, I knew she was right that I wanted her to make it all okay. It was hard to admit to myself, but I knew it was true.

I could hear Frank's voice in my head. *Maybe if you went in there with a positive attitude, you could actually make a difference.* Was he right? If I had a more positive attitude, would that have made a difference in my conversation with Maggie? Somehow I sensed it would have only led to having a bed tray thrown at me.

I could hear the minister's voice in my head, telling me the universe gives us what we want. That we create our own reality. Was this really a reality anyone wanted? Was it God's will and we just had to accept it, as Mrs. Buford claimed? Did we only need to be saved by Jesus, as the minister in the born-again church had preached, and as Susan, our previous MS patient had believed so fervently?

I sighed deeply. If there were any answers, I had no idea what they were. But I slowly began to stop shaking. I finally was able to call the nurse and check on Maggie. The nurse told me that Maggie had calmed down after I left, that she still had not gotten out of bed, but her mother was with her now and that seemed to have cheered her up a bit. I was relieved to know I had not sent her into some kind of nervous breakdown.

The rest of the day was quiet. I visited several patients, checked in a new arrival, and gave a tour of the facility to some prospective "customers." The strange thing about nursing homes is that they have this reputation as places where the same people sit endlessly, doing nothing, but in reality there is a high activity level and fairly high turn-over rate. Things are always moving—people coming and going, so to speak. People going is just a part of everyday life, so much so that we always kept a daily list of deaths on a white board in the front office. It was only for the staff's information, but it always startled me a little bit when I saw it, kind of like a daily calendar with an added note, "Oh, and by the way, these people have left the planet today." Just another block to fill in on the daily planner.

Towards the end of the day, I was tired, and decided it might be a good time to stop in and see Mrs. Avery. If nothing else, I could sit quietly next to her and relax a little.

I walked into the room to find the shades drawn and the nurse fiddling with the equipment next to her. I sat down gratefully, the darkness of the room immediately putting me into a calm state. It was quiet in the room, with just the sound of humming machines. I took a deep breath.

"Oh, no," I said suddenly. I knew immediately what was happening. There is a certain odor that comes over patients as their bodies are preparing to die. It is unmistakable.

I looked at the nurse. She nodded. "It's for the best," she said quietly, stroking Mrs. Avery's arm.

"I know," I said. But not today, I thought. I can't do this today. "Is her son coming in?"

The nurse shook her head. "He said to call us when she's passed."

"Really?"

"Well, she won't know if he's here anyway," she said doubtfully.

"Of course she knows," I said. "On some level." I suddenly realized how important these levels were to me. On some level she knew. I was sure of it. Maybe on this level, she was in a coma. But on that other level, wherever it was, she knew that her only child wasn't here, that he couldn't be bothered to be with her when she died.

I sat back in the chair. The nurse continued moving the tubes around, almost as if she were looking for something to do, a reason not to leave Mrs. Avery alone.

I didn't really know Mrs. Avery. All I knew of her was the little that was in her chart, a social history taken before I had worked at the nursing home. She had been a teacher once, and then a housewife. She'd been married forty years until her husband died of cancer. Her only son had moved two thousand miles away and visited once a year. That was the extent of my knowledge of Mrs. Avery. I hardly seemed to be the one to be sitting at her bedside when she was dying. And yet here I was.

I began imagining what Mrs. Avery's life might have been like, filling in the gaps. I pictured her as a young child with a dog she loved, running through fields. Didn't everyone run through fields back then? I pictured her as a teenager on her first date, a horse and buggy coming to pick her up. Wait a minute, that couldn't be right. She wasn't *that* old.

It was hard to imagine the life of someone you barely knew. But it kept coming to me anyway. I could see her walking home under the stars on her first date. Maybe it was like a scene out of *It's a Wonderful Life.* Now that seemed more like the right time frame. I saw her getting married, getting pregnant, the joy of having her first baby. I pictured her trying to have more kids, the disappointment in not being able to.

It was like I was having Mrs. Avery's near death experience, watching her life pass before my eyes. I didn't know her life, and yet I did. It was everyone's life, the same experiences we all have in one way or another. That was what I was seeing as I sat there.

For some reason, I pictured her at a large Fourth of July party, friends and family around her. She sat in a lawn chair, her husband beside her, her son playing nearby. She was a pretty woman, her face, of course, completely different from the pale, creased, falling one in front of me now. She had dark hair in a kind of old-fashioned wave and big brown eyes. I realized that I had no idea what color Mrs. Avery's eyes really were because I had never seen them open. But in my vision, they were big and brown with dark lashes curled expertly around them.

I sensed her excitement as she watched the fireworks, the display lighting up the sky in a way she had never seen before. I had a feeling come over me as I watched with her, the feeling that in spite of everything, in spite of all her regrets and disappointments, it was all okay. She reached for her husband's hand, and he smiled at her.

Could Mrs. Avery have known back then that one day she would be here, dying alone in a nursing home? Could she have foreseen that her friends and family would be gone, that her son would be far away, and that the only people around her would be a caring nurse and a hapless social worker? What would her younger self have felt if she had known this was her fate? Could she have still felt joy, still reached for her husband's hand with the sense that it would all be okay in the end?

I leaned forward and touched Mrs. Avery's hand. Tears came suddenly, before I even had time to realize they were there. They were already flowing down my cheeks. The nurse looked over at me.

"I'm sorry, "I said. "I know this isn't very professional." I sat back in the chair again, as sobbing started to overtake me. I brought my hands to my face.

I felt the nurse come up behind me and touch my shoulder. "I'll leave you alone a minute," she said. I nodded as I heard her leaving the room.

I couldn't stop crying. It wasn't just for Mrs. Avery, of course. It was for Mrs. Avery's son and her dead husband. It was for Maggie and Mrs. Wellington and Mr. Halloran. And most of all, it was for me. It was for how much I needed to feel like everything was okay and how much I just couldn't feel that it was.

I left the room before Mrs. Avery died. I checked her chart the next day. She had lingered for several more hours after I left. There were jottings as the nurse checked in on her every fifteen minutes to a half hour. And then at 7:30 that evening, this note: "Unable to obtain vitals. Doctor pronounced patient dead by phone."

And so went the final note of Mrs. Avery's life.

Chapter Eleven

"Are you sure we're not going to be on TV?" Sharon asked me as we were walking into the large auditorium. "I would seriously die if anyone from work saw me here."

"We're not going to be on TV," I told her. "But if we were on TV and someone saw you, they'd have to be watching the show, wouldn't they?"

"I guess," she said. "Or they could just be flipping through the stations and they'd see me and oh my God, I'd be so embarrassed."

"This is not one of those guys who is on TV," I assured her.

We gave our tickets at the door and made our way to our seats. Sharon gasped when she saw we were in the third row. "How much did you pay to see this dude?"

"More than I could afford," I said.

She shook her head as we sat down. "This is crazy, Nora," she told me. "What are you expecting to find out?"

"I don't know. Anything would be fine."

"What do you mean—anything?"

"I mean I just want to see what he says."

We waited as others made their way to their seats, and then after a few minutes, a hush came over the crowd as a woman came out on the stage.

"I want to welcome everyone to this very special event," she told us. "For those of you who have never been to a Guy Marlowe session, you're in for a very special treat. Guy continues to amaze us all with his ability to talk to those who have passed on, so much so, that he will soon have his own show on cable."

"Oh my God," Sharon said out loud.

I nudged her with my elbow. "It didn't happen yet," I whispered. "We won't be on tonight."

"Make sure all electronic devices are turned off," the woman was announcing. "We don't want any interruptions at the wrong moment."

Sharon and I reached down to our purses to turn off our cell phones. "We wouldn't want anyone who's actually *alive* trying to contact us," Sharon said sarcastically.

"And now I'd like you to all join me in welcoming Guy Marlowe!" the woman called as she turned and clapped enthusiastically for the man walking out onto the stage. The audience joined her in the applause.

Guy Marlowe was such an average looking man that I couldn't believe he was actually someone who could talk to the dead. I wasn't sure what I'd expected—a long robe, a beard, a halo? But he was just this guy with a regular haircut, khakis, and a polo shirt.

"We'll get started right away since I've already got a crowd here trying to get my attention."

The audience laughed, maybe just a little apprehensively.

"I need everyone to remain open. Even if you think the message is not for you, it could be. You may think of something later that fits, even if it doesn't seem to make sense at the time. Now remember, I'm just the messenger. You don't want to shoot the messenger."

The audience laughed appreciatively.

"Are you thinking he'll talk to you just because we're so close to the front?" Sharon whispered.

I shrugged. "I hope so."

"Okay, in the back rows," Guy was calling out. "I have a gentleman here with a beard, an older man, and I think there's something with his heart." Guy held his heart as if it were hurting him.

"Oh, that's a stretch," Sharon whispered loudly. "An old man with a heart problem."

"Shhh," I said.

"I believe he crossed recently," Guy was saying. No one was claiming this poor man.

"Let's see," Guy said, stroking his chin as if he had a beard. "I'm getting a J or a G. A Jim or George."

A woman called out tentatively. "My father was Gene," the woman said.

"I think I'm with you," Guy said.

"Oh God," Sharon said to me, "Jim, George, Gene, Joe, anything will do." The woman in the row ahead of us turned to glare at us.

"Sharon would you shut up?" I whispered angrily.

"He's standing behind you with his hand on your shoulder," Guy continued. "Did he have a heart attack?"

"No, he had a stroke," the woman said, sounding disappointed.

"I'm not with you," Guy said suddenly.

"What?!" Sharon said, again much too loudly.

"That proves he's for real," I whispered. "He's not just going with anything."

"Well, that woman is expecting George or John to show up," she said.

"Gene," I reminded her.

"Whatever," she said.

"I thought the name was important."

She glared at me.

Meanwhile, Guy was busy with another woman down the row, whose grandfather was a Jim.

"Yes," she kept exclaiming.

"He's talking about a garden in the backyard that he used to love so much."

"Yes," she said.

"He liked to grow roses," he said. "He says he developed quite a green thumb in his old age."

"Yes," she agreed, nodding her head enthusiastically.

"And you're worried about your own health. Something to do with your thyroid."

"Oh my God," the woman exclaimed. "I haven't told anyone."

"Oh, she's planted," Sharon said to me. At least she had the decency to whisper now, even if it was loudly.

Guy was moving on. Another Jim, who wanted to take the opportunity to get in on the Jim bandwagon, and then Gene ended up coming back, though he had very little to say. I suspected that Guy was just trying to make the poor woman feel better after he'd abandoned her so abruptly.

Finally, he moved down into our section. I held my breath. Sharon noticed. "Are you expecting one of your patients to come through?" she asked.

I shook my head. "I hardly think they'd interrupt their heavenly rapture to come visit me."

"I'm sensing an R, a Ruth," Guy was saying now.

The woman on the other side of me gasped.

"My grandmother was Ruth," she called out. Damn, I thought.

"I'm with you," he said. I tried to keep my face pleasant, slightly disinterested, kind of like the expression an actor would have on the Academy Awards when someone else's name is called. But I was pissed. I wanted a reading. Especially after I'd paid all that money.

"Ruth is with you all the time," he was telling this woman, who began crying softly. "She sends her love. And she wants you to know that she sees how you keep the ring she left you in a box on your dresser. She wants you to wear the ring and not guard it so carefully." The woman nodded, crying into the tissue that she had obviously brought in preparation for just such a moment.

I could feel Sharon next to me taking a breath, about to open her big mouth. I elbowed her as hard as I could without making it obvious to Guy who was still looking in our direction. She shut up.

He moved on now, and I sighed. He went around the room, again making it over to a couple of rows behind us. Each time he brought up a name or an image, I wracked my brain, trying to figure out a way it could apply to me. But it never did.

It was amazing how all of these dead people still had the same issues they had when they were alive; they still held the same grudges, still gave the same advice. They still worried about the same stupid stuff. I didn't get it. Did we not really go to sit on some cloud next to God in a state of unending peace when we died? Did we just continue with the same petty lives we'd lived on earth? Somehow it was more comforting to me to believe I'd continue my own pathetic life. I couldn't think of anything more frightening than to spend eternity on a cloud in a state of some kind of moronic haze of joy.

Sharon had finally become quiet, her doubts seemingly quelled by the amazing success this man was having with guessing just the right thing to say at just the right moment.

She leaned over to me. "Nora, I don't understand this," she said, finally whispering in the volume she should have been using all along. She almost seemed embarrassed by her doubts now, whereas earlier she had announced them with complete confidence. I had to smile at that.

"I don't either," I told her. "It's freaky."

"Freaky is not the word for it."

It seemed to go on for a long time, but in reality it was only about two hours. And then it was over. I never got my reading.

Sharon was quiet as we walked out with the rest of the crowd.

"You can't really believe all that," she said finally, as we reached my car and were away from all of the other people.

"I don't know," I said.

We got into my car and I started the engine.

"I don't understand who you were expecting to come to you," she said. "You don't know any dead people except the people you've worked with."

"Yes, I do," I said. "My grandmother."

"Your grandmother's still alive."

"Not my mother's mother," I said. "My father's mother."

"You knew her?" Sharon asked in amazement. "You barely know your father."

"Well, I met her," I told her. "When I was about eight, my mother took me to see her. I think my mother must have been feeling guilty about my father, about my never seeing him. I think she thought it was because of her, that he hated her so much he'd rejected me. Something like that. So she took me to see his mother in a nursing home."

"Ahh," Sharon said. "Now it all makes sense. The nursing home."

"I guess there's a connection," I said, though I wasn't so sure. "She had broken her hip, so she wasn't that sick. I don't even think she was that old, come to think of it." I was trying to remember, but it seems she was older than my other grandmother, maybe much older. It was hard to tell when I was eight.

"So how did she react to you?" she asked.

"Oh, she was funny," I said, as we started out into the dark night. "She smoked non-stop. I think they actually let her smoke in her room. Either that or she was doing it illegally. She went on about my father, how he was a total son-of-a-bitch who cheated on my mother."

"She told an eight-year-old that?"

"Well, she wasn't exactly grandmotherly, I guess. But I liked her. My mother let me visit her once a week for a couple of months while she was there. Then she went home and I went to visit her at her house one Sunday."

I thought of that Sunday I'd been at my grandmother's house. She lived in this little bungalow-type house, the kind that looks like it might blow over if a strong enough wind came along. It smelled of smoke and some kind of perfume. Every now and then over the years I'd smell someone with that same perfume—I never knew what kind it was—and I'd think of this woman I knew for such a short time. She made me barbeque ribs and curly fries for dinner, not exactly what you expect when you think of a home-cooked meal at Grandma's house. She drank glass after glass of wine and talked about her three husbands, all of whom were dead now.

"All sons-of-bitches, every last one of them," she told me, "just like your father." I was fascinated with this woman who told me things my mother never would, and who acted like I was her peer, rather than her long-lost granddaughter.

"So what happened to her?" Sharon asked.

"Well, she ended up back in the nursing home with another broken hip. They called us one night to tell us she had died, an unexpected stroke."

"They called your mother instead of your father?"

"No, they called me. I guess she listed me as next of kin, since my father could never be found. She forgot to tell them I was an eight-year-old."

Sharon was silent a moment, considering all of this.

"So this is the woman you expected to come back from the dead to talk to you?"

"Well," I said, hesitating, "she's the only dead person I'm related to."

We were quiet again and then Sharon snorted. "I don't think she'd be telling you about the ring in the box on your dresser."

"No, but she could have told me she stashed some cash somewhere."

"More likely she stashed bottles somewhere," Sharon said.

"Yeah, I guess you're right." It should have been a joke, but neither of us laughed.

We were both silent now. I looked out at the night as I drove. There was a light spring rain falling and the windshield wipers swished quietly back and forth. It felt somehow like they were trying to comfort me, as if the sound could make all the sadness insignificant, just a little background noise on an otherwise happy life.

I remembered being at my grandmother's graveside after the funeral. My mother took me. It was just the two of us, several women my grandmother played poker with, some ninety-year-old distant cousin who kept shouting at me to speak up, even when I wasn't saying anything to him, and the minister who kept calling my grandmother Jean when her name was Jane. Even at eight years old, I remember thinking that my grandmother was the loneliest woman I'd ever met.

"You know," Sharon was saying. "I don't know if I believe any of that crap he was doing." She sounded more like her old self, less in awe of the mystery of it all, and more sure of her skepticism. "But as went on, I had this feeling of peace come over me. Even when those dead people said the stupidest shit."

"I know what you mean," I said. "I felt it too."

"What do you think it was?" Sharon asked.

I watched the wipers clear the windshield in front of me, back and forth, leaving a light trail of rain, even as they wiped it away.

"I think it was just the feeling that life goes on, no matter what, good or bad, happy or miserable, dead or alive. It just keeps going on."

"And that's a good thing?" Sharon asked, like she really wasn't so sure.

I paused. "Yeah," I said. "It is."

I dropped Sharon off at her apartment building and then made my way home. After Barney's walk, I called my mother.

I could hear the shock in her voice when she realized it was me. I have to admit, I didn't often call her.

"Oh, Nora, I'm so glad to hear from you," she told me. After all the preliminaries of how we were and the weather and how much we'd liked our Christmas presents from four months ago, I finally brought up why I'd really called.

"Mom, do you remember Grandma Jane?"

She was silent for a minute.

"What in the world?" she said finally. "Where did this come from?"

I just went to see a guy who talks to dead people, I wanted to tell her. But of course I didn't. My mother never did well with anything that didn't fit into her mainstream perception of the world.

"I was just thinking about her and I don't know. I just never knew much about her."

"Well, there wasn't much to know, Nora. You remember what an awful woman she was. I often regret letting you meet her."

"Really?" I said. "I never regretted meeting her."

"No, of course not. You thought she was the greatest thing you'd ever laid eyes on. I never understood it."

"Well, she was interesting," I said. "Different from anything I'd ever known."

"I certainly hope so," my mother said. "Listen, let's not talk about her." Of course not, I thought. Why would we want to talk about something real?

"There was this woman at the nursing home who died," I told her, pushing the issue. "And I just realized how alone Grandma Jane was when she died. And I realized how little I knew of her."

"Really, Nora, you're twenty-five years old. Why would you be thinking about old age and death?"

"Maybe because I work in a nursing home, Mom. It tends to come up now and then."

"Don't get smart with me," she said. "I know where you work. You need to get out of that place. Go out and live your life. Find yourself a nice young guy to have fun with." My mother's answer to everything.

"Okay, Mom, gotta go now. Barney's whining at the door."

"Oh, and that dog," she said.

"Catch you later." I hung up. I remembered why it was I never called my mother.

Chapter Twelve

*D*iane was standing outside Maggie's room as I made my way towards it.

"How is she?" I asked.

She smiled but with a worried expression on her face. "About the same," she said.

"So she's still not getting out of bed?" I asked.

She shook her head. "No, they're in there now adjusting her or moving her, trying to keep her from getting bed sores. She asked me to wait out here. I guess she doesn't want another lecture on why she would even be getting bed sores." Diane gave me a sad smile, as if all that were left for her were lectures.

"Well," I said. "No one seems to be able to convince her. We've all tried."

The aides came out now. "You can go in," one of them told us.

Diane touched my arm. "Listen, I'm going to go get some coffee. Why don't you go on in and I'll be there in a minute?"

"Sure," I said with as much false enthusiasm as I could muster. I'd been hoping Diane would be the buffer for me since I hadn't seen Maggie since she'd thrown me out of her room. But that was not to be.

Diane headed off and I turned towards Maggie's room. I knocked hesitantly and stuck my head in.

"Maggie?"

She looked up from a magazine she was reading. She motioned for me to come in. I walked in and stood near the door, not sure what kind of reception I was actually getting.

"Nora," she said, sounding conciliatory. "I'm so sorry."

I breathed a sigh of relief. "Don't even worry about it," I said.

"No, really," she said. "I was horrible to you. I just—" She hesitated. "I just don't deal with things very well sometimes."

"Who would?" I asked. I went over and sat in the chair next to her bed. I could tell from the look of it that it was getting lots of use. All kinds of people had been sitting there trying to convince Maggie to get out of bed.

"Well," she sighed. She hesitated. "Sometimes I go to a dark place, and I don't know how to get out of it." She glanced at me, as if she were trying to gauge whether I would understand. I only nodded.

She sat back against her pillow. "Did you know that aliens are overtaking the earth tomorrow?"

"What?" I asked, startled.

She held up her magazine. A tabloid.

"You read that stuff?" I asked incredulously.

"Oh, this does wonders for my dark places. Nothing pulls you out of a funk like a story in the tabloids."

I shook my head. She was a mystery to me. "Maggie, are you ever getting out of bed again?"

She sighed. "Listen, it's not that I don't want to get out of bed. But Nora, I'm dying."

I hesitated. Was she serious? "Maggie, you won't die from MS. You can still live a full life."

She snorted. "It depends on your definition of full."

"But the doctor and physical therapist think you still have plenty of good years. I mean, maybe you could even go into some kind of remission again." It was a stretch, but anything was possible. I mean, we create our own reality, right?

She shook her head. "When you have a disease like this, Nora, one of the things that you can't help but learn is how to listen to your body. My body knows. It's tired. It's telling me that it's time. There is no point in physical therapy or drugs or any of that."

"But Maggie, that's crazy. Why would you think that?"

She sighed. I could tell she thought I was hopelessly brainwashed by the medical personnel. "When I first got this illness," she said. "They told me I could live a normal life for many years. And I did live a fairly normal life for a few years. But I always knew. Always. Whenever things were about to get worse, my body would tell me. I would feel it coming. My doctor told me I was crazy. My husband told me I was hallucinating. My friends told me I was negative. Even my mother, the mystic that she is, would tell me I should listen to the doctor. But I always knew."

"So maybe you're just getting worse again. That doesn't mean you're dying."

She gave me one of those slightly exasperated, slightly sympathetic looks, the kind that makes you feel like you have just said the most stupid thing possible.

"Nora," she said, motioning around her with her hand, the fingers bending unnaturally even as she did it. "There isn't much worse to get at this point."

I sat back in the chair. How could I reason with her?

"You're the one who likes to think we have levels of awareness, aren't you?" she said, nodding over towards her comatose roommate. "Isn't it possible that my body has a level of awareness that I don't? Isn't it possible that we have wisdom inside of us that goes beyond the logic of doctors?"

"Yes," I said. "But it's a positive wisdom. It's the ability to heal. It's the ability to create a better reality. Not to just give up and die."

"So you're expecting my roommate over here to get up and walk out the door any day now?"

"Well, of course not," I said. I hesitated. What were even arguing about? Somehow I sensed that this was not the kind of conversation a normal social worker would be having with one of her patients.

"I wish that life was always about creating something better," she said. "But sometimes it's just not."

Diane walked in right at that moment.

"Am I interrupting something?" she asked, looking from one of us to the other. I had a feeling that I had a stricken look on my face and tried to brighten up a little.

Maggie shook her head. "I was just giving Nora some life lessons," she said, holding up her tabloid. She smiled over at me, which I somehow understood was a warning not to repeat our conversation to her mother.

Diane was shaking her head. "Those stupid magazines," she said. "I've tried to tell her for years that nothing in there is true, but she just won't believe me."

They both started laughing at that. "You mean the aliens aren't coming?" Maggie asked, sounding almost genuinely disappointed, as if she were ready to accept any way out of this reality right now. "I was so looking forward to going to Neptune."

Diane was holding two cups of coffee and brought one over to Maggie's bed tray.

"Starbucks?" I asked.

"Yeah, there's a new one right around the corner. Have you seen it yet?"

I shook my head.

"If you think I'm drinking that crap they have over by the kitchen," Maggie said. "Do they use that to try to bring people out of their comas? I can't even taste it. It smells so bad, I gag before they even set it on my tray." She glanced at the coffee on her tray. "This isn't a large," she said suddenly.

"If you think I'm helping you to the bathroom every five minutes, you're crazy," her mother said. In some ways they were just a mirror of each other.

"I think I'll leave you two to talk," I said, getting up from my chair. "I've got some paperwork to catch up on."

"Hey, Nora," Maggie called to me as I walked towards the door, as if she'd just remembered something. "What Beatles girl are you anyway?"

I sighed and turned around. Diane smiled knowingly, as if she'd been through this before.

"I don't know, Maggie. This is so stupid."

"What do you mean, it's stupid?" Maggie asked with mock indignation.

"Being a Beatles girl. What difference does it make?"

"Oh, come on, Nora, humor me. I'm sick, remember?"

"Well, seeing as how you're lying in bed in a nursing home, it would be a little hard to forget."

"I can't believe you're playing the sick card," her mother said.

Maggie just grinned. "Come on," she said.

"Okay, I'm a Ringo girl." They both started to laugh.

"Nobody's a Ringo girl," Maggie said.

"What do you mean? I can be a Ringo girl."

"Let's put it this way. A Ringo girl wouldn't know who Ringo is."

"I just wanted to be different," I admitted sheepishly. "He seems different."

"Oh, he is," Diane said laughing.

"That's okay," Maggie said. "Just keep working on it."

I shook my head in resignation. "I guess so," I said.

"Humor me," Maggie called as I left the room. I could hear Diane laughing.

I walked down the hall, thinking about what Maggie had told me. Her body was telling her she was dying? What could be crazier than that? Maybe a man who claimed to be talking to dead people?

Chapter Thirteen

I was attending a weekly meditation class at the church. I don't know why. The prosperity class had done nothing for me. If anything, it increased my poverty. It seemed the more I said my affirmations, trying to convince myself of my prosperity, the more the bills came in. First, a light on my car came on and it turned out to be faulty wiring. It was easily fixed, but still—it was the principle of the thing. Then I got a nice letter in the mail about some old credit card from college that I hadn't even realized still had a balance. The company informed me that they had finally tracked me down and I owed them $200. It was unbelievable to me that they would find me at this exact time—right when I was trying to experience prosperity. But apparently this was the way it worked for me. When I'd told Frank about it, his theory had been that my subconscious mind was bringing all of my negative beliefs about money to the surface so I could release them. I wondered if it worked the same way with relationships.

I wasn't really much better at meditation, but it seemed like the thing to do. It was supposed to lower my heart rate and decrease my stress and give me inner peace. So I attended faithfully, waiting for all of those things to happen.

It was there that I ran into Frank the week after our argument. It was a free class, open to all who wanted to attend, but he normally didn't so I was surprised when he was standing near the door when I walked in.

"Nora," he said, as if he'd been expecting me.

"Frank," I said, definitely not expecting him. Then we just stood there, neither of us knowing what to say.

"So," he said.

"Well," I said at the same time. We laughed at our clumsiness and then fell back into a heavy silence.

"So I guess things aren't really working between us," I said finally.

"I hadn't noticed," he joked.

"Listen, I'm sorry I got so angry. I don't know why I get like that."

He smiled. "Maybe this meditation class will help you with those negative feelings."

And there it was again. Just like that, he pissed me off all over again, just when I was trying to apologize for my last outburst. He was so patronizing. He couldn't apologize. He couldn't admit to anything. It was all me.

Luckily, the class was starting and we moved apart before I could blast him again. He sat on the other side of the circle from me. That was a relief. I couldn't think of anything worse than trying to meditate with Frank sitting next to me thinking how much I needed it.

The man leading the meditation—Bob or Bill or something like that—told us to sit comfortably in our chairs and relax.

"*Breathe deeply,*" Bob began saying, as we all settled in. Or was it Burt? "*Let the breath fill you all the way up and then let it out. That's it. Nice and easy.*"

He reminded me of my mother's boyfriend who took me out driving when I got my temp. "Nice and easy," he kept saying as I'd approach a curve. "That's it."

Even when I'd take the turn a little too quickly, he'd grab the dashboard, and say, "That's it" in a very soothing voice, though it was obvious my turn wasn't even close to nice or easy. He was still trying to impress my mother at that early stage in their relationship, so he never lost his cool with me. It got to the point where I'd take the turn as fast as I could just to see if I could rattle him. He'd look a little green, and his hand would be gripping at the dashboard desperately trying to find something to grab onto, but somehow he'd still be saying, "That's it. Nice and easy. That's it." I started to wonder if he had a recording in his pocket that just kept going off whenever he touched the dashboard.

"*I want you to imagine the ocean,*" Bill was saying, or maybe it really was Bob. I was becoming obsessed with what his name actually was. I saw the ocean in my mind.

"*The waves are coming in, nice and easy. That's it.*" Oh God, I thought, why won't he stop saying that? I didn't want to keep thinking of my mother's boyfriend from so long ago.

"Think of the ocean as your life. Think of the waves as your opportunities. You don't want to choose just any wave, but wait for the right one."

The thing about Frank, I thought, as the waves all rolled right over me, was that I could never just say what I felt. He always had to correct me; he always had to be above whatever I was feeling or thinking.

"Here comes the perfect wave. Embrace it with the joy of your being." I felt the waves just crashing over me, one after the other. I couldn't embrace one of them; I couldn't even tell one from the other. How could you possibly choose the right one?

I wished for once Frank would just say, "I know exactly what you mean." But maybe he never said that because he never did know what I meant.

"You are one with the wave," Burt was saying. I am not one with the fucking wave, I thought. I don't even want to be one with the fucking wave.

I thought of my grandmother on my mother's side. She was like Frank, only much worse. If you said, "The sky is so blue today," she would say, "I think there's some pink over there." If you said, "I'm tired," she'd say, "You don't seem tired to me." If you told her, "I loved that movie," she'd respond, "I've seen so many better movies than that." When you set a fork on the counter, she told you to put it in the sink. If you set a plate in the sink, she told you to leave it on the counter.

I spent a week with my grandparents one summer and I was so tired by the end of it, I could hardly think at all anymore. And I was only ten years old. I wasn't doing all that much thinking anyway, but it was still too much for my grandmother's taste. After that, whenever my mother would suggest I stay with my grandparents, I'd make up excuses. I think that was just as well with my grandmother. She didn't seem to appreciate me any more than I did her. I once overheard her telling my mother I was "high strung" and "unusually sensitive." Unusually sensitive? I guess that's what she called people who had the audacity to express anything at all around her.

My grandfather was silent most of the time. I understood why. It was so rare to hear him speak that I didn't even recognize his voice when he called me once. That one occasion was when I graduated from college. I could hear my grandmother in the background, egging him on, well, actually supplying all of his side of the dialogue. He was so proud of me; I was lucky my mother was so poor that I had received all that grant money; what in the world would I do with a degree in social work? Then my grandmother had to get on the line because she hadn't heard any of my responses. She seemed flustered, like it hadn't occurred to her that by having my grandfather do all of the talking, she wouldn't have the opportunity to dispute everything I said.

My mother would slink around my grandmother, at times trying desperately to please her, then at other times doing things that she knew would piss her off. I could see now why my mother seemed so desperate to find a husband. She needed someone else to tell her who she was, just like my grandmother had always done. Or at least she told her who she wasn't. But then my mother would invariably pick the bad boy, the kind of man my grandmother would despise. Like my father.

"You can let yourself float in this ocean of energy," Bob, Bill, or Burt was saying. How did we get into an ocean of energy? I thought. I had missed the whole ride on the right wave. *"Just let it flow gently over you while we listen to the music,"* he said in a soothing voice. There was a shuffling noise, and some loud clicks on a CD player. How are we supposed to maintain our meditation through this? I thought irritably. Not that I was exactly maintaining a meditation. The button was finally pushed and soft flute music filled the room.

But then there was this one time with my grandmother when I was about seventeen. My grandfather had a heart attack. It seemed to take most people by surprise. He was so quiet and mellow that no one could imagine what kind of stress would bring him to this. My mother was distraught. Her sister and her husband came immediately from their home a few hours away, and they all stood around wringing their hands and whispering in corners. But my grandmother seemed her usual self. Why was everyone so upset? she wondered. My grandfather didn't take care of himself. Of course he'd had a heart attack. Why were the doctors so incompetent? she asked repeatedly. Didn't they know how to treat a basic heart attack? Was it not the single greatest cause of death in this country? She was sure she had read that recently in *Readers Digest*. Did they think he had some kind of exotic disease they couldn't treat? And on she went.

Then one day my mother dropped me off in front of the hospital and went to find a parking space where she didn't have to pay the ridiculous fees the hospital parking garage charged them all, as my grandmother put it. My grandmother thought it a travesty that they would try to make a profit off sick people, and she forbid any of us to park there. Her son-in-law ignored her, of course, but no one ever let on. My mother, trying to be the obedient daughter in the middle of a family tragedy, would spend half of her visit driving around the streets trying to find an empty space that she didn't have to pay for.

I went up to my grandfather's room that day after my mother dropped me off and was surprised to find my grandmother the only visitor in the room. Her back was to me as she sat in the chair next to my grandfather's bed, and his eyes were closed. He seemed to be asleep, or doped up from the medication he was on.

"Tom," I heard my grandmother whisper. "Not now. I'm just not ready." And then she leaned her head onto his chest and began to sob. I was shocked. I had never seen any emotion from my grandmother, and certainly nothing like this. I backed out of the room and stood in the hallway until I heard her stop. She only cried for about two or three minutes and then there was silence. I coughed loudly and waited a second. Then I nonchalantly banged the wall and walked through the door again.

My grandmother was already sitting up, her usual self, my warning signals apparently successful.

"Well, if it isn't our long lost granddaughter," she said sarcastically, which of course I knew meant that she didn't feel I'd been to the hospital to visit often enough, as in every day. As a busy high school senior, I did tend to skip a few days between visits. "We thought you'd run off and joined the circus."

"Not yet," I said.

My grandmother was staring at me, and I knew she realized I'd seen her crying. There was no indication at all on her face, no watery or red-rimmed eyes, no tear streaks, no expression of sadness. But when I looked in her eyes, I saw something different. I saw a look of something that I can't quite explain. Maybe it was trust? Or respect? Or camaraderie? Whatever it was, she knew I had discovered her secret and that I was going to let her keep it.

Not long after my grandfather's heart attack, my grandparents moved away for their retirement. Not to Florida, of course, which my grandmother claimed was filled with all of those "old, tired people, playing cards and putt putt." No, being the maverick that she was, my grandmother had decided they should retire in Arizona. I hadn't seen them as much over the last few years, and I never saw that look in my grandmother's eyes again. I wasn't sure she even remembered the incident anymore, but I did. I never forgot the day I discovered my grandmother had feelings.

"Let's begin to come back to this reality now," Bob was saying. His voice startled me. I was in a different reality, but not in an ocean of energy. I was back in my grandfather's hospital room.

"I'll begin counting back from four. Four . . . three . . ." My eyes flew open. I could see that everyone else's eyes were still closed. Was it impossible for me to follow directions? Could it be that I was like my grandmother? I shivered at the thought.

"And one." The other eyes opened now. Everyone looked around the circle, trying to gauge the others' reactions. I could see what they were all thinking. Had everyone gone into the ocean of energy? Did they find the right wave? Did I pick the right wave or should I have waited? And what was with that flute music? It was like a meditation competition. Who had found the most peace? Who really knew the secrets of the universe?

The others started to talk quietly among themselves, but I stood up to go. I'd had enough. I had never realized how stressful meditation could be.

"Nora," I heard Frank's voice calling me as I reached the door.

I turned around as he came up to me.

"I just wanted to say goodbye," he said and reached out to hug me. He held on for a minute. "I hope you find everything you're looking for in life," he said finally into my hair. He sounded so genuine that it threw me off for a second.

"Thanks, Frank," I said hesitantly as we backed away from each other. "You too." We smiled a little shakily at each other, and then I turned to leave.

Damn, I thought as I went out the door. Couldn't he just be a full-fledged asshole? It would make everything so much easier.

I headed towards my car where Barney Fife was waiting patiently—or not. He was sitting in the driver's seat as I approached, staring at the steering wheel as if he would be taking the car for a spin as soon as he figured out which gear to put it in. I nudged him as I got in, and he moved reluctantly over to the passenger seat.

"That was rough, Barney," I told him as we pulled out and got on the highway towards home. "I don't think you're going to be able to help me with this class." I glanced over at his head sticking out the window. I could see his face in the wind, eyes crazed, ears flowing back, mouth wide open, tongue hanging out with drool trickling down the windshield. He may have been a whiz at prosperity, but he was no Zen master.

We took a long walk when we got home. It was getting to be late spring, but the nights were still cool, and I loved the fact that no one else was around. The dark coolness had scared everyone back into their houses. I could see TVs shining out the windows as we passed, the colors flickering into the dark night as the images changed quickly. I loved to glance inside and see full bookcases and decorative lamps, sometimes a computer at a desk or a blanket over the back of a couch. Rarely did I see any actual people in the windows, only the vestiges of their lives. Maybe they were all stretched out on their couches, out of sight, or rustling in their kitchens during the commercials. But seeing the warmth of living rooms as I walked in the cool night, pulling my jacket closer around me, made me feel like I was walking towards home, and it would only be a short time until I found it.

Barney and I stopped at the schoolyard, and I let his leash drop to the ground as I sat on the swing, watching him. He rushed around, sniffing in corners and behind bushes, rooting out old candy wrappers and stones as if they were small animals he was hunting. He would grab them between his teeth and carry them around triumphantly, a huge find in the wilds of the schoolyard. I slowly rocked in the swing, not going into a full stride, but just gently gliding it back and forth.

I thought about the prosperity class, and meditation, and creating my reality, and Frank's belief that I was too negative. All I seemed to know for sure about any of it was that I couldn't manufacture my feelings. I tried to do it the way they said I should, and I just couldn't. None of it seemed to be working for me. And I didn't know where to go from here.

Barney Fife was standing at the top of the slide, staring at me uncertainly.

"Go ahead, Barney. You've done it before."

He started gingerly down the slide, and then started to lose control of his feet. He was panic-stricken for just a second, and then he let loose, running down it with complete abandon, his four feet flying in different directions, his butt bouncing up and down, his tongue hanging out. I knew if he could talk, he would be squealing with joy, shouting out to me about how this was the best thing ever. He landed with a thud at the bottom and looked up at me, panting with complete satisfaction.

I walked over and picked up his leash. "Come on, Fife," I said. "Let's go home."

Chapter Fourteen

I was surprised to see Maggie sitting in her wheelchair when I walked in her room.

"You're up!" I said with enthusiasm.

"Yeah," she agreed with much less enthusiasm.

I sat down across from her. "So you're back in physical therapy?" I asked hopefully.

"Yeah, I went and let her move my legs around in a few circles. Vicky was thrilled."

"Valerie," I corrected her.

"Vicky, Valerie. Same kind of cheerleader name."

"Do you have something against physical therapists?" I asked.

"I just don't like doing things to please other people," she said with some irritation, but more resignation. "So now Vicky can go home and tell her boyfriend that she saved me, that without her help, I'd just be lying in bed, or whatever it is that she needs to tell him. I just don't like being responsible for other people's meaning in life."

"I think Valerie really is just trying to help."

"Of course she is," Maggie agreed. "You're all trying to help. So I'm sitting up in my wheelchair to get everyone off my back. In the long run, it's easier to just give them what they want. I don't have the energy to fight them anymore."

She did look tired, exhausted really. And frail. Much worse than when she had first checked into the nursing home only a few weeks ago. But maybe it was from being in bed too much. Maybe now that she was up and moving around a little, she'd start to regain her strength. I realized I was now resorting to giving myself a pep talk since I knew Maggie wouldn't want one.

"So let's not talk about my illness," she said. "I'm so tired of talking about that. What's happening with that young man of yours?"

I had to smile at the old-fashioned way she said it. I didn't want to break it to her, but I thought she might be hanging around these old people too much.

"We broke up," I told her.

She nodded like she'd been expecting it.

"I don't know," I said. "I mean other than being the most passive-aggressive person I've ever met, Frank's not a bad guy."

Maggie chuckled at that. "Sounds like quite a catch."

"I mean, he really is a pretty good guy. It's just me. I think I just want to be alone for a while."

Maggie nodded. "That's okay," she said, as if sensing that I needed permission.

"Relationships are just so hard," I continued, as if Maggie were confused and had asked me to explain it all to her. "So much is expected of you. So much is demanded of you. And I feel like after a while, I just start to disappear. Do you know what I mean?"

She nodded and spread her arms out. "Why do you think I'm sitting in this wheelchair when I don't want to be?"

"Oh," I said, suddenly seeing it in a different way. It seemed like because we were trying to help her, it was okay to keep pushing her. But then again, hadn't Frank always claimed he was trying to help me too?

"You know, I never loved my husband," she said suddenly.

"Really?" I was so surprised.

She nodded. "I was relieved when he finally decided to leave," she admitted. "And the poor man. He felt so guilty. Leaving me when I'm so sick? I tried to reassure him. I tried to tell him it was for the best. But what could I say? I want you to leave? I never loved you anyway?"

She paused. "It really was a dilemma. Would it be better for him to live with the guilt of leaving me or the pain of knowing his wife never loved him? I couldn't make that choice. I just defaulted to the guilt." She paused again. I could tell she was really considering it. "Maybe that was a cop-out. I don't know. Maybe I just didn't have the guts to tell him the truth."

I wasn't sure what to say. Maggie sat quietly, her head down, thinking it through. "Maybe I should write a letter to give him when I'm gone."

I hated it when she said things like that, but I knew she'd be furious if I tried to correct her.

"Why did you marry him if you didn't love him?"

She looked up, startled out of her reverie.

"Well," she said, as if launching into an epic story, one she had told many times, though I could tell she had really not talked about this much at all. "I don't know."

That was her epic.

"You don't know?" I repeated.

"I mean, I know that I was thirty and I thought it was time to get married. Everyone was getting married. And there was Michael. So I married him."

"Now that's a romantic story."

Maggie laughed. "Of course I told myself all kinds of things that made me believe I loved him. He was a great guy, so good to me. My parents liked him. My friends thought he was wonderful. I really thought I loved him. But then, we were about eight months into the marriage. It was all fine. Everything really was fine. You know, I think that was it." Maggie paused and considered that for a moment. "It was all seemingly fine. But then one night I woke up in the middle of the night, sat straight up in bed and thought—my God, what have I done? It was all fine, but it was not at all what I wanted."

"What did you want?" I asked.

"Oh, you know the usual things. To travel the world. To live in Paris and be an artist. To fall madly in love with some Frenchman who would beg me to stay there with him." She laughed, delighted with herself. "Nothing realistic, of course. But that wasn't really it. I mean, by thirty I knew those things weren't going to happen. But I wanted something else, something more. That's all I knew." She paused. "And then the next week, I was diagnosed with MS."

I took in a sharp breath.

"Yes, that wasn't exactly the 'something more' I was looking for." She laughed, but not with bitterness, more with a sense of wonder at how it had all played out.

"Is that why you didn't leave?"

She shrugged. "I don't know," she said again. "It might be. I started to tell myself again how great he was and how it was all fine. And maybe it was." But she looked unconvinced. "I didn't know what to do at that point, and neither did he. So I stayed. And stayed. It was just easier to stay than to leave."

"Hmm," I said. "I don't seem to have that problem. It's much easier for me to leave than to stay."

Maggie smiled. "I think it's better that way," she said. She looked sad, forlorn almost. "You know, I didn't do anything in my life that I really wanted to do. I always just went along, did what was expected of me. You probably find that hard to believe, don't you?" She looked at me expectantly.

"Yeah, I do," I said. "You're quite the rebel now."

I could tell she was pleased with that label. "Until today," she said reluctantly. "I gave in to defeat." She seemed to truly believe that she had lost some sort of battle for her soul by agreeing to get out of bed.

"A small concession, don't you think?" I asked.

She nodded, thinking it over. "Yes, I guess you're right. But I have so few choices any more, you know?"

"I know," I said, with an overwhelming sense of sadness, but it seemed to be only a practical matter to Maggie. This was something she should have done for herself and didn't.

"When I think back on it all, I don't know why I didn't make more choices. Why I didn't do the things that mattered to me when I had the chance. Of course, I didn't know I would end up like this." She looked at me. "It's probably different for you, being around all of this every day. But most of us, when we're young and carefree, we don't think of what can happen. Of how your life can change so drastically and go in ways you never expected."

I nodded. I thought of it every day, but I knew most people didn't. Even older people like my mother, who you would think would have gotten used to things by now, were always so shocked and dismayed when people actually got sick, or even more appalling, died from their illnesses. They were offended by aging, by the fact that people could no longer walk or hear or even care for themselves. So they pretended it wasn't happening; they told themselves it would never happen to them. I guess I could consider myself one of the "lucky" ones, who already knew by the age of twenty-five what was going to happen to all of us.

"Love is so strange," Maggie said suddenly, interrupting my train of thought.

"What do you mean?"

"I don't know," she said. "It just comes at the wrong times sometimes. And then you think it will come again, and it doesn't. And you wonder."

She seemed lost in thought, so I just waited for her to tell me what she was talking about.

"I loved this guy in college," she said, her eyes lost in some long ago memory.

"So what happened?"

"I was so young, and everyone told me to wait. To get a job and be on my own. You know how it was in the '80s." She looked at me briefly and checked herself. "Well, no of course you don't. But it was a time when women were finally coming into their own, and you were supposed to go out and build a career, and wait to have a family, and all of that. There was a lot of pressure back then to figure it all out." She paused. "I suppose there still is, but I just don't care anymore."

"So you wanted to get married?"

"I wanted to be with him. It wasn't really about marriage. It was just about him. But you know, at least back then, it was all supposed to lead somewhere and if it didn't, then you had to move on. "

She paused again, her eyes jumping with the memories.

"Ahh," she sighed loudly. "I didn't know what I was doing. If only I had thought this all through back then."

"Better late than never, I guess," I said lamely, and cringed at my own stupid remark. But she didn't seem to notice.

"Oh, but I loved him," she said again, as if I hadn't caught that. "His name was Brad. Such a typical name, isn't it?" She laughed at herself. "Doesn't everyone have a Brad in their life?"

"Not really," I said. But she didn't hear me. I don't think she remembered I was in the room anymore.

"We broke up when we graduated. I was heartbroken. But I thought— I'll fall in love again. That's what everyone said too. You'll meet someone else when you're ready. The right one and all that." She laughed, almost bitterly. "There is no 'right one.' There is no perfect guy out there, no soul mate. There's just the guy you love, whoever he might be, you know?"

I could only shrug. I had no idea.

"Well, there is. I just had so many expectations about how it was all supposed to be. And I thought love would come again. But it didn't. And you just never know."

She looked at me and seemed to come back into the room, back to the reality of the nursing home, and away from her lost love.

"What do you think my chances are of finding my soul mate here?" she asked suddenly.

I laughed out loud. "Well, Mr. Halloran would certainly be interested."

She snorted. "Do you know that man wheeled himself up to me and made kissing noises? It was disgusting."

I sighed. "I didn't know, but I'm not surprised."

"Well, it's nice to know I've still got it," she said, pushing her short hair away from her face in a fake sweeping motion.

"Listen, Maggie, why don't we try to find Brad?"

Maggie shook her head and looked sad, not so much for herself, but for me. "Oh, Nora," she said. "It's way too late for that. Brad is married and has four children. I hardly think he's going to leave his wife for a dying cripple."

"He doesn't have to leave her. You could just say hello, tell him how you really felt back then, that kind of thing."

"We both knew how we felt back then. It doesn't matter anymore." She shook her head, as if to chase the thought away. "This is just what happens when you get older. Even at my relatively young age." She laughed. "It's not all MS, you know. There's this thing called a mid-life crisis. Unfortunately, I can't go out and buy a red Ferrari and find a hot young hunk." She chuckled at her own joke. "But you start to wonder at what might have been. You'll see one day."

I frowned. That actually sounded almost more depressing than old age.

Maggie laughed at the look on my face. "It's not all that bad," she said. "You just take stock of your life, think about how you want it to be different. It's a good thing, really."

"Okay," I said doubtfully.

"Listen, help me back to bed, will you?" she said suddenly. "I'm really tired and could use a nap."

"I don't really do that," I told her. "Let me call the aide."

"Oh, for God's sake, are you kidding? Do you think I want a twenty minute lecture on why I need to extend myself, and keep trying to maintain my quality of life? Why would anyone want to maintain this quality of life?"

I hesitated. I thought about what she had said about making choices in her life. She was making one now.

"Okay," I said. I wheeled her over to the bed, and she stood up. I supported her as she maneuvered herself onto her side and then lay flat on her back.

"Ahh," she sighed loudly. "That feels great." She lay back and closed her eyes briefly. Then she opened them again, and reached for my arm. "Hey, you've been great. Thanks for listening to all of that. I don't know what came over me."

I could only smile. For once I felt like a real social worker. Like a good social worker.

I left Maggie to her nap and went down to the nurse's station. I hesitated when I saw the nurse on duty was Helen, an older woman who could be patronizing. But then I launched into my spiel anyway.

"You know, Helen," I said. She looked up from whatever it was she was working on at the desk. "I think it might be a good idea to let Maggie make her own choices about getting out of bed or not. I think I'm going to put that in her chart."

Helen stared at me blankly for a minute, but then it seemed to register with her what I was doing. I was being a social worker.

"And why do you think that?" she asked with just the slightest note of an attitude, one that let me know she thought social work might be a useless profession, and that a young social worker in particular, might not have any idea what she was talking about.

I soldiered on in spite of her implications, feeling quite brave. "I think Maggie needs to feel a sense of control in her life. She needs to know that she can be respected for her choices."

Helen let out the slightest snort. "Well, put whatever you think you need to in the chart. We'll see." With that, I was dismissed. I started to turn away. For a split second, I thought about turning back around. There were so many things I wanted to say, all of them completely unprofessional. I told myself I was taking the high road, but the truth is, I just didn't have the guts to say any of it. So I walked away.

I felt a small pinch on my butt. I flew around.

"Mr. Halloran!" I exclaimed angrily.

"Gotcha!" he said like a little boy, a mischievous look in his eye.

"You know—" I started and then stopped. What was the point?

Instead, I took hold of his wheelchair and started pushing him back to his room. He seemed pleased with the attention, which after all, was what he really wanted.

"Mr. Halloran, was there anything you wanted to do in your life that you never got to do?" I asked him as we wheeled companionably through the hallway. Other wheelchairs lined the path, with residents who were nodding off or staring blankly, and some carrying on complete conversations with themselves. One man shouted at us to stop, that we were under arrest. It was like we were in some kind of weird parade, Mr. Halloran and I, and we just kept moving forward, ignoring the distractions.

"Like what?" he asked suspiciously.

"I don't know—something you wanted to accomplish, a dream you've always had?"

He shrugged. He seemed so genuinely puzzled that I felt bad for even bringing it up, like I was a teacher asking him a question in front of the class and making him look foolish for not knowing the answer.

"Nah," he said finally. "What's there to do that I ain't already done?"

We walked silently for a minute, surrounded by the sounds only a nursing home can make—loud talking, clanking bed pans, whirring machines.

"Nothing," I agreed finally. "There's nothing else to do." And the parade went on.

Chapter Fifteen

"Ahh, finally you show up," Mr. Gordon said as I came into his room. He was right. I'd been avoiding him. I just didn't want to hear about any more wars.

"Hello, Mr. Gordon," I said as loudly as I could.

He was sitting at his typewriter, a very large pile of cleanly typed pages beside him. He leaned back in his chair thoughtfully, holding a cup of coffee as if we were about to have a nice chat.

"Ahh, kiddo," he said. "It's all too much for me."

I was slightly alarmed, though I should have known better. "What's too much for you?" I asked, taking the bait.

"First Korea, then Vietnam."

I groaned, but he couldn't hear me.

"Why is that too much for you?" I yelled, sitting down in his armchair. I decided I might as well make myself comfortable for this foray into Mr. Gordon's world.

"So many conflicts for America to be involved in. And for what, you might ask?" I wouldn't, but he was going to tell me anyway. "There were no real benefits for this bloodshed. And then the Gulf War. Don't even get me started on that."

That seemed like a good idea. "Mr. Gordon, what about your personal life? Aren't there some personal stories you'd like to tell in your book? After all, it is your autobiography."

"Oh, but it's all personal," he assured me. "The war affected all of us in ways we weren't even aware of."

"Which war?"

"All of them, of course. Going over into these other countries. And our men dying. Everyday, our men dying for their country."

"Well—" I tried to interrupt, but he was still going.

"And the evil of it all."

I sighed. "Which evil would that be?" I wasn't even going to guess this time.

"The evil of communism, for God's sake. The spread of communism was the biggest threat to our country in the last half of the twentieth century."

I was confused, and in spite of myself, I felt compelled to clear it up. "But you said there were no benefits from going to war."

"What?"

"You said the wars were useless," I shouted.

He held up his hand as if to stop me from saying another word, a look of complete alarm on his face. "Useless was not the word I used!" he spit out. "The problem is we did not complete our task. We were not able to root out communism, and thus the wars went on. The evil continued to spread."

I leaned back in my chair with resignation.

"When I think of those young men coming home in wheelchairs, all shot up, disabled, mentally confused, broken in so many ways. The terrible tragedy of war. I feel compelled to tell my story."

"What about your wife?" I asked suddenly.

"She was a lovely woman." He didn't seem thrown off his rhythm at all by my sudden change in the direction of the conversation.

"Are you writing about her in your autobiography?"

"Yes, her brother was in World War II, and she had a nephew who was actually killed in the Korean War. If we'd been able to have children, our sons would have served as well."

It was hopeless. Mr. Gordon would never see his life through any other lens.

"Now the Korean War," he continued, as if I'd never mentioned his wife. "That was an interesting one. Of course, in the context of the other wars, it hardly registers as a conflict. You know, it's not really known as a war?"

"No," I said. "I don't know that." Did I care?

"Ah yes, but we must consider it in the context of the other wars. The threat of communism, of course, was such an important aspect of the wars of the last half of the century," he repeated.

"Uh-huh."

"The Korean War should have given us a better idea of what we would face in the Vietnam War."

"Uh-huh."

He paused. I took that as my opening.

"Was your wife as interested in these things?" I asked as loudly as I could.

He stared at me.

"What things?"

"The wars," I said, with some exasperation.

"Oh, heavens no," he said. "She never wanted to hear about the complexities of it all." I couldn't imagine why. He chuckled as he thought about her. "She had her opinions, of course." He paused, and I thought I had finally reached him, I had finally figured out how to get him to talk about something else. But it didn't last, of course. "She never understood the Vietnam War. Now that's going to be at least three chapters, if not more. The social context of that war." He shook his head in disbelief.

"Well, your book sounds very interesting," I lied. I stood up to go.

"Wait until I get to the Gulf War," he said with excitement.

I nodded and tried to smile, but I think I grimaced.

"I'm thinking of calling the book *The Twentieth Century War*," he said. "What do you think?"

"But there was more than one war."

"Pff." He brushed his hand in front of his face as if this were ridiculous. "It all seems like one long war to me."

I had to agree with that. It *was* one long war to him.

He began walking me to the door in his gentlemanly way. "I'm realistic about finding a publisher," he said as if I were trying to convince him that his book would be a best seller and he wanted to contain my excitement. "I'm not sure anyone is interested in hearing what an old man like me has to say, but we'll see." It was true. I was not at all interested in hearing what an old man like him had to say, but my need to escape overrode my pangs of guilt.

"Yes, well, it can be difficult to get published," I said as if I knew all about it.

He patted my arm. "We'll see," he said in a comforting tone, though who he was comforting, I'm not sure.

I left his room and went to the nurse's station. I was relieved to see the nurse on duty was Cathy, the one who had given me a toy for Barney.

She was measuring medicine into small cups at the counter, but turned towards me as I walked up.

"Cathy," I said. "Do you think there is any way we can get Mr. Gordon to focus on something besides war?"

She shook her head. "I don't think so. It's the biggest regret of his life."

"What is the biggest regret of his life?"

"Well, he was too young for World War I and then I think he was really too old for World War II, though he tried to enlist anyway. They wouldn't take him because of his asthma. It's like he missed out on the most important events of his lifetime. You know, the Greatest Generation and all that."

"Oh," I said, suddenly surprised. "How do you know this?" I couldn't understand how she would know something as a nurse that I wouldn't know as a social worker. After all, she took care of the body while I took care of the mind.

She shrugged as she lined the medicine cups on a tray. "There's something about changing bedpans and cleaning up puke that lets you know people in a way that maybe others don't. I mean really—is there anything more intimate?" She chuckled to herself at the thought.

"Oh," I said again. I felt humbled suddenly by the idea that changing someone's bedpan was a higher calling than delving into their psyche. I stepped away from the desk, a little shaken.

"Don't let it bother you, Nora," Cathy said, somehow noticing my reaction in spite of her attention to what she was doing. "Mr. Gordon enjoys talking to you because he can keep up his façade. He can pretend he's a dapper old man writing an important book, and not someone who needs a nurse to remind him to take his pills every day. "

"I guess that all makes sense," I told her reluctantly. But I still felt like I had missed something important. I turned to go.

"Hey, how does Barney like that rabbit?" Cathy called after me.

I turned back to her and smiled. "Loves it," I told her. "Makes him feel very prosperous."

She looked a little puzzled at my choice of words, but she seemed pleased.

That night I had a dream. I was in a war, of course. Where else would I be? It was chaos, with soldiers running everywhere, guns blasting, and huge explosions. I tried to run, but I couldn't. I simply stood staring.

In front of me were two figures. To my left was Mr. Gordon, standing in a stooped position, holding a large rifle. To my right was Maggie, sitting in her wheelchair, holding a pistol. I looked from one to the other, confused.

"The world is at war," said Mr. Gordon. "And there's nothing you can do."

"Disease will overtake you," said Maggie. "And there's nothing you can do."

I opened my mouth to say something, but nothing would come out. I kept moving my mouth, trying to speak—I don't even know what I wanted to say—but there was only silence.

Finally, a deafening noise surrounded us, as debris fell from above and the ground rocked below. A bomb had exploded.

"We're all dying," Maggie yelled.

"Humanity has learned nothing," Mr. Gordon shouted.

I lost sight of both of them as the force of the explosion propelled me off my feet and onto my back. I lay there, staring up at a sky I couldn't see through the smoke and black dust that lingered.

"There must be something more," I whispered to myself, finally able to make sound come out.

I sat straight up in bed as if I had just heard a blood curdling scream, and not my own quiet voice. I was sweating profusely and shivering at the same time. The whispering left me with a creepier feeling than the loudest scream.

Barney rolled over from his perch next to me on the bed, his legs socking me in the side as he sighed deeply in his sleep. I glanced at the clock. It was 3:14 am. I lay back down and stared at the ceiling for two hours before finally falling back to sleep.

Chapter Sixteen

I kept beating on my drum like I was told—boom, boomboom, boom—trying to get the feel for it. A woman I'd met at the meditation class, Jessica, had talked me into going to this drum circle. It had seemed like a good idea to try something with activity and movement, anything but just sitting still and feeling the oneness, or not feeling it, in my case. I didn't really get what it was all about, but from what I could see so far, we all sat in a circle around a blazing fire in the parking lot of the church and banged on drums or shook rattles. One man even had a tambourine.

We were told to just get into the rhythm of it as we felt it move through us. I closed my eyes and tried to feel the beat. What immediately came to mind was that song one of my mother's boyfriends used to sing—that drummer guy named Matt or Mark or something. He'd always come in the door singing some dumb song he loved, something about not working and banging on a drum instead. My mother would laugh every time. Every damn time, even when he did it over and over.

This boyfriend never had any money, and my mother would buy him things, and pay some of his bills. She even paid his rent one month. It got to the point where I just wanted to say, "Dude, maybe that's the problem! Go get a job already and stop banging on your stupid drum all day." But my mother thought he was "amazingly creative." She was even getting ready to let him move in permanently, until he decided to sell our VCR for some extra spending money. She finally dumped him after that. Something about him messing with her movies made her crazy.

She was funny that way. She would let things go forever with people, mostly her boyfriends, putting up with all kinds of bad treatment, and then something that seemed minor in the relative scheme of things would set her off and that would be the end for her. The guy would be shocked that this one little thing would piss her off that much, never seeing it coming. I never saw it coming either. It was always as surprising to me as it was to them when she would suddenly kick one to the curb.

The tambourine man was letting loose. The loud jangling sound was annoying, especially as it seemed to explode around us. I didn't really understand if we were supposed to all be on the same beat, but we obviously weren't, especially the tambourine. I didn't know what that guy was trying to prove, but his beat was really messing me up. Did he have no sense of rhythm?

I'd asked Jessica what exactly a drum circle was. I'd gotten some kind of mumbo jumbo about how it was finding the internal rhythm of the universe and thus connecting with our inner selves. I don't know how I always ended up trying to connect to the universe. And why wasn't I already connected to the universe? It was all very confusing to me. I was hoping that one of these days we could just pray to God, you know that white-haired guy who created heaven and hell, and sent his only son and such. It seemed like a much easier concept to wrap my brain around.

The church was located on a fairly busy street, and people were honking as they went by. This was somewhat embarrassing to me, but luckily the fire did not light up our faces enough for anyone to recognize us. We could remain anonymous. Anonymous drum beaters in a loving universe.

I had a kind of pathetic drum actually. And I had only one stick. But still, I gave it my best shot. One boom, then another, then a series of booms, trying desperately to find the internal rhythm of the universe. But it was impossible with that damn tambourine!

The man was almost directly across from me in the circle, and I finally looked over at him, ready to face off with him, ready to give him my most evil eye. But he was looking at me already, as if he were prepared, as if he already sensed my annoyance. In the firelight, I could just barely make out what I thought was a glint in his eye. And then he gave me just the slightest smile. I paused a minute, taking it all in. I sensed a renegade in our midst.

I began to beat on my drum to his rhythm. It was difficult at first because he was all over the place, but gradually I began to sense some sort of atypical beat and I was able to follow it, a step behind at first, and then, slowly, subtly, I could feel it just a split second ahead. I glanced over at him and his smile now was a little broader, but still sly. He didn't want to give away our secret.

I could feel the discord in the rest of the group. They weren't sure what was happening exactly; they just knew their beat wasn't working as they thought it should, that the universe was not providing them with the internal rhythm they sought. Instead, they were grasping, trying to find a harmonious beat and failing. It was an unbelievably powerful feeling. This man had led me over to the dark side so easily. Just like that, I was willing to disrupt the internal rhythm of the universe. What did that mean about me?

Another car honked as it passed and some teenage boys hung out the window. "Hey, anyone want to bang me?" one of them called out.

The group went on drumming, as if they had heard nothing. I glanced over at the tambourine man, but he only continued on with his irregular beat. As I was apparently the only immature drummer in the group, I coughed to cover up my laugh and looked down at my drum as intently as I could. I tried to think of the saddest movie I had ever seen, but nothing was coming to mind.

Unfortunately, the teenagers had decided to turn around and drive by again. I guess the banging metaphor was too good for them to let go.

"Hey, baby, I got a real big drum you can bang!" one of them yelled this time.

I held my hand with the drumstick in it to my mouth. I tried so hard not to snort, but it was impossible. I glanced quickly at the tambourine man who had a broad smile on his face.

There seemed to be some rustling around me, but it was hard to tell with all of the racket from the drums. The man leading the circle spoke up. "Let's focus, people!" he called out.

But it was way too late for me. My shoulders shook and my stomach hurt from trying to hold in my laughter. I turned away from the group and pretended to be having a coughing fit. When I turned back, the tambourine man was laughing openly at me. It was all his fault. First, he had led me astray with the beat and now I was laughing inappropriately at teenage boys' stupid jokes. There was no hope for me. I knew I should feel guilty, but for some reason all I felt was relieved. Finding the internal rhythm of the universe was just too heavy of a burden to carry.

I was able to get control of myself, and the banging—on the drums, not the teenage boys—went on for a while. Then one by one, people began to stop drumming. I noticed that the leader of the group stopped, and I was going to stop with him, but I noticed the others were continuing. I wasn't sure what I was supposed to do. Then, slowly, one by one, people quit on their own until there was silence. The group sat quietly for several minutes. I was so thankful that there were no more shouts from the passing cars.

"Does anyone want to share their experiences?" the leader finally asked in a hushed tone, as if he had just entered a funeral parlor.

Several people did.

"My heart was filled with love for all of you," one woman said. "I could feel that we were all part of this white light, so loved by the universe, so cherished." She smiled as she looked around at each of us. Oh my God, I thought, what in the hell is she talking about?

"I was filled with such a sense of peace," one of the men said. "I could feel the rhythm of the universe just moving through me." I couldn't understand it. Did he not hear the loud and obnoxious tambourine, or the loud and obnoxious teenagers for that matter? But it seemed that all that didn't fit into the perfection of their universe was ignored.

And on it went, until all the bliss was exhausted. And so was I.

I walked back to the car with Jessica. She was what I guess most people would describe as very spiritual. She wore a mu-mu and dark eye-liner. I wasn't sure why dark eye-liner was a requirement for spiritual women, but they all seemed to wear it. Her hair was long and flowing and encircled her like a kind of New Age halo. You felt immediately that she would pull out tea leaves and read your future, and in fact she would. Well, tarot cards actually. She was a somewhat well-known psychic in the area.

"I'm sensing a disconnect with you, Nora," she said. I was startled that she picked that up so easily. She didn't even have her tarot cards with her.

"I did have some trouble getting into it, you know, the whole drumming thing," I said.

"Why?"

"I don't know," I said, pausing. "I guess it just felt kind of forced."

"In what way?"

This was aggravating beyond words. Because I had no words. I had no way to describe why none of this made sense to me.

"Because I don't see how sitting around banging on a bunch of drums does anything for the world," I said finally.

"Ahh," she said. "So that's it."

"So what's it?" I asked.

"You feel somehow responsible for the world."

"No, I don't feel responsible for the world. I just—I just don't think it's this simple."

"You don't think what is this simple?"

"I don't know," I said. I sighed much louder now, much more obviously. We had stopped next to Jessica's car in the parking lot and were facing each other. Why had I let her talk me into coming to this in the first place? I couldn't even remember why we had struck up a conversation at the meditation group. She'd sat next to me, and after the meditation, she'd suddenly started talking to me about all the different things she was involved in, and then the next thing I knew she was telling me how I had to come to this drum circle, how it was an amazing event. And now here I was. Just like with the tambourine man, I was so easily persuaded. It annoyed me to see that about myself.

"But Nora," she was saying. "It's about finding our bliss. It's about expressing ourselves in the highest possible way. Whether it's drumming or dancing or meditating, or whatever it is that makes your heart sing, that is what we have to do to give ourselves to the universe."

I felt like I was floating when she talked, like my brain was disconnected from my body and was just hanging in the air, in a state of limbo, I guess you could call it, but not really on earth anymore. I was pretty sure this was the way she was feeling and I was picking up on it. Which one of us was the psychic anyway?

I shook my head, trying to bring myself back to reality. "But what if you're not expressing yourself in the highest possible way?" I asked, hearing my own frustration. "If all this world is about is floating around in a state of bliss, then why doesn't anyone else seem to be in on it?"

She shook her head just as I had, as if she were trying to shake away my dark state of mind, just as I had been trying to shake away her bliss. "Oh, Nora," she said. "I sensed this same disconnection from you at the meditation class. You're too much in the world. Remember, we want to be in the world but not of the world."

I stared at her. I'd heard that before, but I had no idea what it really meant. I wasn't sure I wanted to.

"Why don't you come for a tarot card reading, and maybe I can help you resolve some of these issues?"

A tarot card reading. Of course.

"I'll think about it," I said as we waved goodbye and I walked towards my own car. As I opened my car door, I sensed a tarot card reading was in my future, in spite of how annoyed I was. I'm kind of psychic that way, I guess.

Chapter Seventeen

Allison, the young nurse about my age, was at the medicine cart outside Maggie's room as I approached. She shook her head to let me know Maggie was not having a good day. She hadn't been having many lately.

I walked in to find her lying in bed, sobbing.

"Maggie, what's wrong?" I said, rushing to her side. She nodded her head towards the wall where the TV was playing. I could see that a movie was just ending. Someone had been able to hook up her DVD player for her.

"Brines" was all I heard.

"What?" I asked.

"Brines on," I heard now.

"What?" I asked again.

"Brian's Song," she spit out.

"Oh." I sat down in the chair next to her bed. I knew of the movie from my mother. She would always ask at the video store if they had it. She told me it was one of her favorite movies. We could never find a copy of it because it was only some old, made-for-TV movie. Then one time we finally found a copy at some obscure video store, and my mother excitedly rented it. It sat at our house for a week because she never watched it. She even paid late charges on it. She said it was too sad to actually watch. From what my mother told me, I knew it was about some football player who died of cancer and somehow this made everyone cry uncontrollably through the whole thing. I wasn't sure what the attraction was of this storyline, but women of a certain age seemed to find it irresistible.

"Maggie, maybe you shouldn't really be watching that kind of movie right now," I said finally. She was still crying, pulling one tissue after another out of the box next to her.

"I'm sorry," she said, but it came out muffled under the piles of tissue she had wadded up to her mouth.

"The doctor thinks anti-depressants might be able to help you," I said.

"I'm not going on anti-depressants," her muffled voice said through the tissue.

"I know," I sighed. I'd already been informed of that.

"Maybe talking about it would help." I knew everything I said sounded rote, like it was taken from some social worker/doctor/psychiatrist/nurse/anyone-who-ever-talked-to-a-sick-person manual. But I didn't know what else to say.

Maggie had stopped sobbing by now and was quietly sniffling into her tissue.

"I'm not sure why I can't be like him," she said.

"What do you mean?"

"I don't know why I can't joke on my deathbed like he did and make everyone feel better. I'm just cranky and difficult."

I was silent. "Not all the time," I said finally, with a smile.

She snorted into her tissue.

"Okay," she said. "I'll give you that."

She sighed deeply and threw her wadded up tissue towards the trash behind me. Of course she missed. I went over and stood next to it, hesitating.

"Use another Kleenex to pick it up," she said in a nasally voice, as if she were talking to a child. I took her advice and was able to throw it out in the most hygienic way possible.

I sat back down, joking, "I'm not here to pick up your snotty tissue," but tears were streaming down her face again.

"So much I missed out on," she was saying.

"What do you mean?"

"Life," she said in an annoyed voice, though I knew she wasn't really annoyed with me. "I've missed out on life. I just wasted it away. Why didn't I move away after college? Somewhere fun and exciting, like I wanted to? Why didn't I go to Europe? Why didn't I travel around the country on a motorcycle and camp under the stars? Why didn't I join the Peace Corps? Why didn't I fall in love for real instead of marrying someone safe? Why didn't I get a dog, for God's sake?"

"Get a dog?" I asked.

"Yes, I always wanted a dog, but my husband hated them. Said they were too much trouble."

"Well, they are quite a bit of trouble," I said, thinking of Barney Fife.

"Yes, but who cares? Does everything always have to be so easy? Why couldn't I have let things get a little messy once in awhile? What is life if it's not messy? What is life if you don't do the things you want?"

I was starting to get depressed right along with her.

"Well, you couldn't have done all of those things, Maggie," I said, thinking this was logical, if not exactly inspiring.

"Why not?" she asked in an accusing voice.

"It would be hard to fit that all in, don't you think?"

"Why?" she asked again.

I hesitated. I felt like I was floundering, which of course, I was. "I mean the Peace Corps and a dog wouldn't work together, I can vouch for that. Neither would riding around the country on a motorcycle, unless you had one of those side compartments for the dog." I smiled at my cleverness.

She laughed fleetingly, but then the tears came again.

"Oh, Nora," she said, "you have no idea how sad I am."

I sat back in the chair and watched her cry. She sobbed quietly for several minutes and then she finally stopped, and was just sniffling into her tissue. She started to aim for the trash again, but I held up my hand.

"Please," I said. I got up and brought the trash can next to the bed so she could simply reach her arm out and drop it in.

"The night nurse wasn't that excited when she found a ring of dirty Kleenex around the can either," Maggie said, chuckling. "It's an old habit, I guess. I was on my high school basketball team. But of course I was a better shot back then." She paused. "A little better anyway."

"High school basketball, huh? Well there's an experience you didn't miss out on."

She smiled. "Those were some fun times," she admitted. "We weren't very good, but we had a blast. You know, in one game I actually made the winning shot?" She looked over at me as if expecting me to nod my head in recognition, like I would have seen it on the evening news or something.

"It was so exciting. We were down by one, and someone threw me the ball. I have no idea why because I wasn't that great of a shot. As you've seen." She nodded over towards where the trash can was, chuckling to herself. "But somehow I ended up with the ball at the last second, so I just threw it up there. And it went in. The crowd—what little of it there was—went wild. I just stood there with my hands on my head, unable to believe it. The rest of the team ran up to me, patting me on the back, congratulating me. They probably would have picked me up on their shoulders, but we were such an uncoordinated bunch, I think they were afraid they'd drop me." She paused, and I could see that she was reliving the moment, feeling it all again. "It's funny, but it really was an exciting moment in my life, as meaningless as it might seem."

I was watching her, thinking of what Jessica had said to me about being of the world, but not in the world. How could you be more in the world than to score the winning shot in a basketball game?

"What are you thinking, Nora?" Maggie asked suddenly, seeing something in the way I was looking at her, I guess.

"Oh, I was just noticing how happy you seemed, reliving that moment."

"Well, it's not quite the same as touring Europe, but it was a special moment in my life," Maggie agreed.

"Were there any others like that?"

"Oh dear," she said. "Isn't this some kind of cliché? A dying woman reliving those precious, yet simple, moments in her life?"

I sighed. She really could be difficult sometimes, there was no denying that. A downright pain in the ass.

"First of all, you're not dying," I said in my best lecture voice, "not yet. But if you insist on being on your deathbed, you said you wanted to be more like what's his name, the happy guy who cheers everyone up. It would really cheer me up if you would stop talking about all the things you didn't do and started talking about the things you did do."

"Well," she said. "Aren't you Miss Social Worker?"

"Yes, I am."

"Okay, let me think about it." She paused, deep in her memories. "Hmm, I guess I would say playing Elaine."

"Elaine?"

She seemed to have forgotten I was there for a minute, and looked up like she was surprised to see me still sitting there. "Elaine in *Arsenic and Old Lace*. In my late twenties, before I got married, I suddenly decided I had the acting bug. Actually, I think a friend of mine convinced me it was a good way to meet eligible men. I'm not sure exactly how. But anyway, we tried out for a community theater production of *Arsenic and Old Lace*. It's an old play. You're probably too young to have heard of it."

"And you actually got the part?" I asked. "You were an actress?"

Maggie laughed. "Not at all, but there were so few people at the auditions that I think it was between me and a woman in her forties, who really wasn't going to cut it. The part was for a young woman. So I got it."

"That's great."

"Yes, well, it turned out to be a lot of work. But I have to admit, I had always had a secret desire to act. I just never had the nerve. I guess that's why it was so easy for Jen to convince me to try it." She paused again. "But it's not really that interesting of a story."

"Go on," I said. "You're cheering me up, remember?"

"Right," she said, as if just remembering that. But she seemed pleased to continue, in spite of herself. "Well, when it came time for opening night, there were *way* more people than I was expecting, that's for sure. And I looked out at that audience, and I suddenly felt so sick. I didn't think I could do it. I thought—what have I gotten myself into? I almost pulled the director aside and told him to forget it, I wasn't going on."

"So I heard my cue and really, I thought I was going to puke right there." She paused and I could see her again reliving the moment. "But somehow when I got out there, something just took over. I was so nervous that I think I just kind of left my body and became the character. Something like that. Do you think that's how Meryl Streep feels?" She laughed.

"I don't know. Maybe."

"Anyway, it was thrilling really. And afterwards we had our cast party, and I got so drunk because I hadn't been able to eat anything all night. But everyone kept telling me how great I'd been in the role." She was smiling, basking in the glory of it all.

"Wow, Maggie, that's amazing."

"It's hardly amazing, Nora. It was just a small part in a community theater." But she was still smiling with pride.

"Did you do any other plays after that?"

She sighed. "No, I met my husband not long after that, and I don't know, it just kind of fell by the wayside, you know. I was so busy and being in a play takes up so much time."

Another regret. I was kind of sorry now that I'd brought it up.

She looked over at me. I must have been cringing because she laughed. "Don't worry. I was never going to be an actress. It was just a hobby. A fun one, but ultimately, just a hobby." She didn't sound completely convinced of that, though. We were both quiet for a minute. I wasn't sure what to

105

say and Maggie seemed to still be caught up in the past, not really paying much attention to my presence.

"It's so strange," she said, staring off into space. "When you're young, you think you have so much time. Well, you do of course. All the time in the world. And then life just happens, you know. You get a job, you get a husband, you get a disease." She chuckled at that as if it were her own private joke. "And then you wake up one day and you don't have so much time any more. It sneaks up on you."

She looked over at me. "Don't let that happen to you."

I shook my head. "Maggie, you still have time."

"Yes, I suppose I do," she said, somewhat reluctantly. "I have some time." She sighed again, and I could see that I was never going to make it as a cheerleader.

"What do you think happens when we die?" she asked suddenly. She threw me off. I hadn't been expecting that question, though I probably should have known this was where it was all going.

"I'm not sure."

"My father was a staunch Catholic. He worried so much about being punished by God when he was dying. It was sad really." She paused, considering it all. "My mother had been what you'd call a sometimes Catholic. She could take it or leave it. After my father died, she just kind of gave up on it. I was never much of a believer either."

I waited as I saw her working it out in her mind.

"When you don't really believe in heaven or hell, there's not much left, you know?" She looked at me as if I had the answer.

"But life goes on," I said uncertainly. I wondered if I should tell her about my trip to see the guy who talked to dead people. But I sensed she wasn't ready for that. Or maybe I wasn't ready for that.

"Yes, I think life does go on. I just have no idea how."

"Maybe just as it is now," I said suddenly. "Maybe nothing much changes."

She frowned at that. "God help me if that's true."

"Well, I mean without your body."

"I suppose," she said with quite a bit of doubt. We both sat silently for a minute, as neither of us knew what the answer was.

"Nora, go on and visit some other patients," Maggie said finally. "You don't have to sit here with me."

"That's okay, I'm fine here."

"That was my indirect way of saying I want some time alone," she said directly.

"Oh, yeah, of course." I stood up, picking up her trash can to put it back.

"You'd better leave that here," she said pointing to the place next to her bed. "And maybe let me know before you come next time, so I can be sure to watch a comedy first." She smiled a little sadly.

"I will definitely do that," I agreed. "I don't want to keep picking up your missed shots."

I left her like that, with her box of tissue in her lap and her trash can waiting beside her bed. It was a vision of her that would be hard to shake.

Allison was at the nurse's station when I went by, so I stopped. Her head was down, and she was intensely focused on whatever she was writing. I waited patiently until she finally looked up at me.

"What are we going to do about her?" I asked.

She shook her head. "I don't know. We all try to make her feel better. But what can you say? I think she's clinically depressed."

"Probably," I agreed, but not really knowing if that's what it was or not.

"You know, I've been attending this church lately," I told Allison. "I guess you could call it New Age. And I'm wondering if some of the stuff they talk about there could help her. Positive thinking or meditation or something like that."

Allison looked around the area quickly, as if she were checking to see who was listening, then put her finger to her lips and motioned for me to be quiet.

"Nora, are you crazy?" she asked, somewhat frantically I thought. "Don't be talking about that New Age stuff around here."

"Why not? People talk about it. Even Oprah does shows on it."

"But this is different. You're a social worker. You'll ruin your credibility."

"What credibility?"

She paused. And then she kind of laughed. "Well, that's true, I guess. But still, I just don't think it's a good idea to bring that kind of thing into the workplace. No one will take you seriously."

"But she needs some kind of help. And I don't know what to do."

"I don't know what to do either. Nobody does. We'll just have to keep working with her, keep trying to get her to a better place."

"I guess you're right," I agreed, but reluctantly. I had been hoping she would offer something more.

I turned to go back to my office. It was always these kinds of moments—the helpless ones—that made the halls of the nursing home seem endless. It was times like these when I noticed the handrails that lined the starkly white walls and the cold echo of my heels clicking on the tile floors. There is just something so depressing about waiting for people to die, however long it takes them to do it.

Chapter Eighteen

aggie was lying on the bed with her eyes closed and her earphones
on. I couldn't tell at first if she was asleep, so I snuck by as quietly
as I could. I'd been neglecting her roommate lately, spending so much
time with Maggie. The curtain was pulled between the two beds, and I
went around it and pulled a chair over next to comatose Mrs. Lowry. As
I sat down, I noted her quiet breathing, her lack of motion. Nothing had
changed since my last visit, of course, and there wasn't much to report on,
but still, it was my responsibility to check in on her, so I did.

I sat quietly with Mrs. Lowry for just a few minutes until I heard
shuffling movement from behind the curtain, then some humming, and
finally a full throated singing. At least I think it was singing. Actually, it
could have been moaning.

I had no idea what was going on. I looked at Mrs. Lowry, as if she
might be able to clue me in, but of course she wasn't exactly reacting to
the commotion.

The moaning or singing or whatever it was went on from there. The
words were all jumbled together and got louder and then quieter, like when
you don't really know all the words, but you're trying to sing confidently
anyway.

Suddenly Maggie's voice was really loud. "Hey, hey, hey what you say,
Sherry Darlin' . . ." she sang.

I couldn't take it anymore. I stood up and walked over to the other
side of the curtain. I stood watching as Maggie, still with her eyes closed,
was what you might call dancing in her bed. She was moving around as
best she could, and her hands were in the air pumping to the beat. I was

just thinking how maybe acting wouldn't have been such a great choice for her, or at least not musicals, when her eyes flew open and she saw me standing there.

She held up her finger to let me know to wait a minute and danced around another minute.

"Well let there be sunlight, let there be rain," she cried triumphantly. "Let the brokenhearted love again…" Some more "la da das" and noise and then finally she pulled off her earphones, still humming. I could hear the beat coming from her earphones, along with the distinct sound of a sax.

"You're disturbing your roommate," I told her.

"Oh, really," she said. "What level of awareness is she being disturbed on?"

"All of them."

Maggie laughed delightedly. "I sound much better without the earphones."

"I doubt that. What are you singing?" I went over to her bed now, deciding that regardless of my responsibilities, this side of the room was much more interesting.

"It's Bruce Springsteen. God, I love this song."

"I know Bruce Springsteen."

"Oh, you don't know this Bruce Springsteen," she said. "This was before he became a pop star."

I must have looked puzzled. "Never mind," she continued. "Just another '80s moment. But you know, Ipods are the greatest invention ever." She held it up for me as if I'd never seen one before. "Do you know I can fit just about every song I ever wanted to hear on this little thing?"

I was staring at her. This was not the same Maggie I'd seen just days before. Was she not clinically depressed, but possibly bipolar?

"What's wrong?" she asked.

"You're just in such a better mood. Did something change?"

"Oh, it's just perimenopause."

"Perimenopause?"

She laughed. "Yes, I tried that on one of the nurses and she seemed to take it all in. No one can seem to understand that MS is an incredibly depressing disease, so I'm just telling them it's perimenopause. Something everyone can embrace enthusiastically."

"We understand that MS is depressing, Maggie," I told her.

"No, you don't," she said. "Not really. But how could you unless you've been through it yourself? Don't worry about it." She pointed to the chair by her bed. "Nora, have a seat. I want to tell you about something." I sat down.

"So, I've been thinking," she said in a very serious tone now, removing her earphones and turning off her ipod. "This can't all be random."

"What can't all be random?"

She motioned around her. "Everything. Life. Disease. Death. All of it."

I had no idea what she was talking about.

"It just seems that there must be something behind it all, you know? I mean not a God sitting up in the sky controlling everything and not some sort of plan that was put into place and we're all just playing our part, but something else."

She leaned forward in her bed as best she could, her body somewhat limp, but there was an intensity to her that I hadn't seen before. "Have you ever had a moment where everything just seems to make sense? Where all of a sudden it all seems very clear?"

I tried to think if I had ever had one of those. "I don't think so," I said.

She leaned back, a little disappointed. "Well, I had one of those yesterday. I don't know if I can explain it, but I was just sitting here thinking about everything—my life, what I'm doing in this nursing home, all of it, and I suddenly saw that it wasn't just a random series of events. That none of it is random for any of us. It's all a kind of work of art, you might say. I guess sometimes it's not very good art, like when I'm looking at my body in my wheelchair. And sometimes it can seem to be brilliant art, like when you're looking at the Grand Canyon. Maybe it's all in your perception, I don't know. But it's all a creation that we're making all the time, all of us, and it's not just happening on a whim. It's life, it's our creation." She looked straight at me. "Do you have any idea what I'm talking about?"

"Do you mean like we're all creating our own reality?"

"Well, yes," she said. "Kind of."

"So you're saying you created this reality?" I asked, motioning around me at the nursing home room, incredulous that Maggie had come to the same conclusion as my church. "This is what you want?"

"No, of course this isn't what I want. I'm not creating it on this level." She smiled suddenly. "Are we back to your levels of reality? On another level, this is all as it should be." She sighed in a defeated manner. "Wow, it all made so much more sense in my head. Now I can't explain it."

I had no idea what she was talking about. What had happened to God, the universe, the light, something I could hold onto? This life as a work of art on a whole other level was too ethereal for me.

111

"If it makes you feel better, Maggie, then whatever you need to believe."

"Oh, Nora, don't start patronizing me now," she said in a pleading voice.

"Well, I don't know what you're talking about."

She sighed. "No, I suppose you don't. You're too young."

"What does this have to do with my age?" I asked defensively.

"When you're young, you need everything to be concrete, etched in stone. It takes a while in life before you realize it's just not that way."

"Well, I need something to hold onto."

"Yes," she said. "You do need that until you realize there is nothing to hold onto."

I wasn't sure if this was coming from her disease again, or if she knew something I didn't.

"Okay, Nora, I won't burst your bubble. You want something you can hold onto. But I just want something that makes sense, that tells me how it really is. I just really need to understand what's going on."

"But how can all of that make sense to you, all of that stuff about life being a work of art? About it all being right on another level?" I asked bluntly.

"Well, how does God make sense? How does it make sense that some creator made this world and put us all down here as some kind of test? I mean, what is he doing? I'm supposed to be a good person and then I'll go to heaven? But what is being a good person? I mean I haven't killed anyone; I haven't stolen—if you don't count the stuff I shoplifted as a teenager. I never cheated on my husband—if you don't count the guy at work I almost slept with that one time."

"Really?" I asked, getting caught up in the scandal.

"You see what I mean? I don't know if I'm a good person or not. I guess I'm an okay person most of the time. So I get to go sit up on a cloud for eternity? That's all this is about? I come here and try not to do all these things I really want to do—well, I can't say I ever wanted to murder anyone, not really anyway—and then God rewards me? Is that all it's about?"

"Maybe it's about getting in touch with the oneness." I was surprised to find myself using the lingo from church. But I didn't know how else to answer her, and I wasn't sure I was comfortable with her theory.

She looked at me with genuine confusion. "What oneness?"

"Umm," I said, fumbling with these concepts that I didn't really understand, "the oneness of the universe and how we're all connected."

She considered that for a minute. "I guess we're probably all connected, that's true. But that still doesn't explain what we're doing here."

"No," I agreed, "but the universe is in charge. We need to let the universe give us what we need."

She stared at me. "Huh?"

"You know, kind of like giving your life to God, but instead you let the universe—" I paused. "You let the universe direct things in a way. If you think positively and try to get in touch with the goodness of the universe, it will all work out."

Maggie scratched her head and frowned.

I sighed. "I don't get it either, but somehow, it's all supposed to flow and be positive and nice, if you can only somehow get in touch with that nice, positive flow."

"Wow," she said. "That's about the biggest bunch of crap I've ever heard."

"You think?" I was so used to everyone else telling me it made perfect sense that I was actually relieved that it didn't make sense to someone else.

"If I just go with the flow and think positively, everything is going to be wonderful?"

My voice had gotten very quiet. "Yes," I squeaked out.

"What planet is that on? I want to go there."

I didn't say anything.

"You mean if I just think positively I'm going to get up and walk again?"

I felt a little ridiculous. "Well, yes—kind of. Theoretically, I guess."

Maggie was silent for a minute, as if she were thinking this over. "If only it were that simple," was all she said.

I couldn't say anything in answer to that. After all, I wasn't the one who would have to get up and walk.

Maggie went on, seemingly forgetting I was even there. "I just wish I would have experienced life more. So much of my life was just going through the motions, and I realize now, that there was so much more going on, that it was all so much more important than I realized."

She stopped suddenly, now just as silent and still as she had been talkative and energetic a little while ago. I waited.

"Boy, that 'Sherry Darling' really takes me back," was all she said as she stared off into space. Finally, she looked over at me. "Well, it's become a habit for me to unload on you."

"It's okay," I told her. "It's kind of my job."

"What a strange job," she said, "listening to people's crazy talk."

"Well, this isn't nearly as crazy as some of the other stuff I've heard."

"Really?" she said. "Do tell."

I had to laugh at her old-fashioned expressions. It made her seem older than she was.

"It's all very confidential," I said. "People's craziness is their own personal business."

"Ahh," she said. "That's no fun." She sighed and lay back on her pillow.

"Maybe you could try getting out of bed again?" I suggested.

She only chuckled. "It must be difficult to be around this much death for all of you who work here," she said as if she hadn't heard me.

"Sometimes," I agreed.

"Isn't it strange how afraid we are to die? We hang on and hang on. We even build homes for people to live in while they're hanging on, and we put them on machines to keep their bodies alive, just so we don't have to admit we're all going to die one day."

"Is that what we're doing here?" I asked, somewhat taken aback at her comment.

"Isn't it?"

I looked around me at the sterile environment. Except for Maggie's personal pictures, and the huge face of John Lennon peering over me, the room did feel like she was already dead.

"I hadn't looked at it like that before," I said, almost guiltily.

"It's not your fault, Nora. We all do it. I'm doing it just sitting here contemplating my life. I'm not living anymore."

I took in a sharp breath. All of a sudden it seemed to make sense. Was Maggie planning to end it all herself? Was that what this conversation was all about?

"Maggie, please don't tell me—you're not considering—" I stopped. I wasn't sure how to put it. "Well, taking things into your own hands," I finished.

"Oh, God no," she said. "I might go to hell."

I had to laugh in spite of myself. "But you don't believe in hell."

"Well, you never know. That would be a horrible way to find out I was wrong."

I put my head in my hands and laughed with both a sense of relief and nervousness, if you can feel both of those things at the same time. Maggie was unlike any patient I'd ever had before, and I had no idea what to do with her.

"I just have to figure out how to live while I'm like this," she said. I peered back up at her. Was this a breakthrough?

"Considering that I didn't even know how to live when I was physically okay, I don't know how the hell I'm going to figure it out like this, but hey, we all have our challenges in life."

"Yes," I said tentatively, uncertain where to go with that statement. "I guess we do." Luckily, Maggie never seemed to notice my stupid responses to her profound statements.

She closed her eyes, suddenly exhausted. I took that as my cue to leave.

Chapter Nineteen

*J*essica's house was on a side street, a small suburban cul-de-sac with older homes and tiny yards. I walked past a beautiful weeping willow tree that took up almost her whole front yard and was standing on her porch, still admiring it, when she opened the door.

"Nora," she said. "I'm so glad you decided to come."

"But I didn't even ring the doorbell," I said, startled by her appearance.

"I sensed you were here."

I tried to check my skepticism as I followed her into her house. More likely she'd heard my car pull up, right?

The inside of her house reminded me of the willow tree—flowing and easy-going, filled with plants and flowery rugs and beads in the doorways. Even the furniture flowed from one piece to the next, an overstuffed couch led to a pillowy chair, and then on to a stereo from about 1989. I recognized it because my mother had one just like it when I was growing up. One of the doors on the double cassette player was missing, but otherwise it looked almost brand new. My mother's was the same way. Something about the shiny black material it was made out of caused it to look eternally unused.

"Have a seat," Jessica said, and I sank down into the soft couch. I loved couches like this. The one in my apartment was small and though the cushions were still in good shape, in spite of Barney Fife's outline being permanently etched into them, I could just never get comfortable on it. Not like I could on one of these couches. That was my dream when I had enough money—to buy an overstuffed couch. I guess you have pretty simple dreams when you're broke.

A slight scent of incense wafted through the air, as soft music played in the background, some kind of chimes, followed by a quiet, monotonous chanting. As I sank back into the wonderful cushions, I felt as if I had suddenly arrived on the soft cloud Maggie was talking about. Maybe she was wrong about heaven. Maybe it was simply an overstuffed couch in a soothing living room.

Jessica was wearing a mu-mu which billowed around her as she sat in the chair next to the couch. Her long, dark hair was loose and flowed around her shoulders much like her dress had settled around her.

"I made some chamomile tea," Jessica said. I tried not to show my distaste as she poured me some. I didn't even like regular tea, so I was sure this would be worse. But I didn't want to be rude.

"Have you had it before?" she asked. I wondered if she "sensed" my dislike of it.

"No, I don't think so."

"Well, why don't you try it? It's very calming and will help you get into a more relaxed and open mood for the card reading."

I sat forward on the couch and took a sip. It was not as bad as I thought, not nearly as bitter as regular tea.

Jessica sat in the chair nearby and picked up a deck of large cards.

"I'm so glad you've decided to try a tarot reading," she said. "I think it can really help you." I was pretty sure the $75 I was paying would help her as well, but I didn't say so.

"Before we get started, do you have any questions?"

"Well, I'm not sure how this works," I said.

"I'll have you shuffle the cards and cut them three times, and then I'll lay out a spread. I think a Celtic Cross would be best for you to start out with."

"But I mean, how do the cards work? How do you get information from them?"

"They're symbolic," she said. "Very much like your dreams. Your subconscious is at work as you shuffle and cut the cards. That's why it's so important for you to do it. Then I help interpret what it is your subconscious is communicating. It's really quite fascinating."

My skepticism must have been showing because Jessica laughed.

"Don't worry, Nora. You don't have to believe in it. It will work in spite of you. Now just focus on whatever it is you want answered in the reading today. It can be anything—work, relationships, romance." She smiled at that, as if romance was always such a nice thing to deal with.

117

"Okay," I said doubtfully as she handed me the cards. I shuffled them as she instructed, but I didn't focus on anything. I didn't know what to ask. I was just hoping she'd tell me something that made sense, something that helped me understand life a little better. I cut the cards into three, like she said, and put them back into a pile to give back to her.

She began to lay them out on the coffee table. She put one down, another on top of it, more around them, and then some at the bottom. I had no idea what it all meant, but it did seem to be in the shape of a cross. I took in a sharp breath when I saw the last two cards. The next to last one showed a picture of a tall building on fire, and all I saw on the last one was the word *Death*, but that was enough to give me a pretty good idea of what it was all about.

"Oh my God," I said, ready to jump up and leave.

"Now, don't worry," she said, a little nervously I thought. "Remember, the cards are symbolic. These don't necessarily mean something bad is happening."

I took a deep breath. "Well, I do work in a nursing home, so I have a lot of death in my life."

"You know, it may not even mean that," she said. "The Death card can simply mean the death of an ideal or a hope, or the death of a part of yourself, maybe even a part of yourself you need to let go of."

Now that's putting a positive spin on it, I thought.

"And *The Tower*," she continued, pointing to the other card, "always just means change. It can be a good change, but it is usually a big one. But let's see how they relate to the other cards."

She pulled up the covered card, the first one she'd put down.

"This represents you," she said. I laughed when I saw that the card was called *The Fool*. There was a picture of an airy-fairy kind of guy looking off into the distance, and he even had a dog with him. It was symbolic of Barney Fife and me, I guess.

"Now this isn't what it might seem," she said. How often would she say that? "It doesn't mean you are a fool. It means you're at the beginning of a journey and you're open and possibly somewhat naïve. But it's a good card overall because it means the world is before you." It was amazing to me how Jessica could make it all sound so wonderful. I thought she really should look into a career in PR or advertising or something like that.

She paused for a minute, and looked up, as if she were seeing something. "I sense this is a spiritual journey," she said. She also happened to know me from a church, so I thought that was a pretty good guess.

She picked up the card that had been covering the first card. "This is what crosses you," she said as she put it back in its place. Again the card was depressing as I saw a couple of pathetic looking people in the middle of a snowstorm—the *Five of Pentacles.*

"You have some money issues," she said matter-of-factly.

"Do I ever," I said. I had to give her that one.

"But this is about more than money," she continued. "It's a poverty of spirit." I sat up straight, ready to defend myself. What had happened to the positive spin?

"I don't have a poverty of spirit," I said, somewhat defensively.

"It's not you exactly," she said, lost in thought, seemingly trying to feel her way through. "You're surrounded by a poverty of spirit which affects you deeply."

"Yes," I said. "As I mentioned, I work in a nursing home."

"It's not just that," she continued. Oh my God, I thought, she's really not trying to make me feel better anymore. "It's those in your immediate circle as well— your family."

"My family?" I asked.

But she was already moving onto the next card, ignoring my comments. She seemed to be on a roll, and my interruptions were hardly worth her time.

"The card above represents what you hope for," she said. I saw *The Star* and was pleased to see that at least my hopes were positive.

"You have high hopes, high expectations, high aspirations which are constantly crushed by the poverty of spirit around you."

"This is really depressing," I said, but she ignored me.

"But there is a strong woman in your background," she said picking up the next card, a queen with a large cup in her hand. "Your mother."

"My mother?" I asked incredulously. Now I was truly shocked.

"But there is another influence that's just passed," she said, moving on.

"Wait, wait, wait," I said rather assertively, holding up my hand. Jessica looked up from the cards and blinked her eyes, as if just waking from a dream.

"I think you have that wrong. That can't be my mother. Maybe my grandmother," I said, thinking of how bossy and overbearing my grandmother could be.

"No," Jessica said with a confidence I didn't understand. "It's definitely your mother. Your grandmother has a false strength she uses to cover up her uncertainty about life."

"How do you know that?" I asked.

"It's in the cards," she said pointing to the spread. Now she motioned around the room. "And it's in the air." And then she pointed at me. "And it's in you."

"It's in me, but I don't know it?"

"Oh, come on, Nora. You know that about your grandmother. She sucks the strength out of everyone around her because she has none of her own." I stopped for a moment to think about it. I guessed that Jessica probably had a point, but I just couldn't understand how she could know that.

"But your mother has a real strength. And you learned from her."

"I just don't see that," I said. "She's spent her whole life looking for some man to take care of her."

"But she raised you by herself?"

"Did you sense that?" I asked in awe, getting into the spirit of it all.

"No, I just surmised it from what you said."

"Oh." I really wasn't getting this psychic thing.

"So she spent her life looking for someone else to take care of everything for her, but ultimately she took care of it all herself."

"I suppose," I said.

I was thinking about how my mother had been the last time I'd seen my father. He had come back around when I was about eleven, all friendly and fatherly, wanting to take me to a ballgame and have dinner. He just kind of appeared out of nowhere. We weren't even sure where he was living at the time, but he said he had come into town for a few days. We all had take-out together at our kitchen table and then sat in our tiny living room watching TV. No ballgame after all. I remembered now how my mother had sent me to bed finally, pretty late for a school night, and said she needed to talk to my father. We lived in a small two-bedroom apartment, so of course I left the bedroom door open a crack and stood listening. I heard my father babbling on about something to do with the child support that month, and then my mother was making a shuffling noise like she was getting out her purse maybe, and finally I heard her say, "Here, take it."

"This is the only time, I swear," he said.

"That's what you said the last time," she told him. I could tell from her tone of voice that she was done. She rarely got to that point with anyone, but when she did, you knew to duck and cover. Sometimes her boyfriends found out the hard way. I wondered how well my father knew her, if he had any idea about this hidden trait in her.

"Listen," she said to him in that tone that meant her teeth were clenched and her jaw was tight. "You're either going to be in her life or out of it. I don't care which it is. But don't you come around here pretending you want to be a father when you really want your money back."

"Okay, okay," he said.

"No, it's not okay, okay. Make a choice and stick to it."

"I really appreciate this."

"Just go," was all she said, and I heard the door close behind him.

My father never came back. He sent me a few more birthday cards, and I'm pretty sure he kept paying child support, maybe not regularly, but enough to keep my mother going. But that was it. Surprisingly, I'd never blamed my mother for his not coming around again. Somehow I knew, even at the time, that she had my back when she told him to make a choice. And he had.

Jessica was watching me. "You see what I mean?" she asked.

"Maybe," I said hesitantly.

"It's not that your mother wasn't strong; she just never knew her own strength."

"Maybe," I said again.

"Okay, let's move on," she said with some resignation that she couldn't convince me. She looked back at the cards.

"I see another woman who you've recently come to know, another woman who is teaching you about strength," she said, pointing to the next card, which I could see said *High Priestess.*

"A priestess?" I asked. It was such a strange word.

"Yes, someone who has much knowledge."

She stopped for a moment and stared off into space. I wanted to glance across the room to see what she was looking at, but I could tell from her eyes that she was focused inside herself.

"This is a woman who challenges you deeply." I knew she was talking about Maggie, but I didn't want to admit it. It was getting eerie how she knew these things.

"Well, she's very sick," I offered finally, as she wasn't saying anything else.

"Yes," she agreed. "But she too is starting out on a new journey, just as you are. The two of you agreed to meet at this time to begin your spiritual journeys together."

"Really?" I said. "What do you mean—we agreed?"

"It was a contract, someone you were supposed to meet in this life."

"You're kidding," I said.

"No," she told me. "It happens all the time. In this case, if the circumstances were right, you agreed to meet as catalysts for each other's journeys."

"So she's going to be alright?" I asked.

"Oh, she's going to be fine."

I breathed a sigh of relief.

"I know you worry about her, but you need to understand that she is finding her own way. Just as you are."

"Okay," I said.

"In fact," she continued, pointing to the next card, the *Page of Wands*, "I believe you'll be getting a message from her in the near future."

"What kind of message?" I asked.

"I'm not sure," she said, shaking her head as if to clear it. "I'm not getting a strong sense of the message, but it will be positive. You'll appreciate it very much."

"Hmm, that's mysterious," I said, now getting into the spirit of it all. It didn't even occur to me anymore to question how she could be so sure about some things and so vague about others. It was just the way it worked. Somehow her staring off into space made me feel that she really was tuning into some frequency I couldn't reach. It was fascinating.

By now, Jessica had moved to the bottom row of cards.

"Well, you're having some issues with conventional religion," she said.

"I'm not much into conventional religion," I told her.

"Yes," she agreed as if she already knew this, which of course she did from my going to the New Age church. "It's more than that."

Of course it was.

She pointed to the first card in the row at the bottom of the cross. "Your attitude is conflicted," she said, and I could see that there was a man on the card with a blindfold on, holding two swords that he crossed in the air.

"The reason I think it has to do with religion," she continued, "is that the next card is *The Hierophant* and that usually has to do with conventional religion."

"What is a Hierophant?" I asked.

She seemed distant, still lost in thought. "It's another kind of priest. Lots of those going on here." She was kind of mumbling, as if she were talking to herself. I waited patiently.

"You know," she said, looking up. "I believe you're struggling with societal conventions. Not just religious or spiritual ones, but all conventions. I believe that this new spiritual journey you're embarking on means letting go of these conventions, finding a new path."

She studied me for a moment. "Even our church is not going to work for you."

I was startled. "Why do you say that?"

"I'm not sure," she said, looking back at the cards. "But you must find your own way, even if that means doing it all by yourself."

"Oh, great," I said.

She pointed back to the earlier cards. "This is why it has been so important for you to learn about strength."

"And so we come to *The Tower* card," she continued, referring to the burning inferno, the one that had scared me so much at first. I felt much braver now, sure that Jessica could make it all turn out okay in the end. "This, of course, is what you fear in life, which is change."

She paused again. "So as much as you need to find your own way, you fear that path, you fear making the change, so you cling to more conventional ideas, anything you can hold onto."

I fell back onto the couch as if she had just hit me.

"God Jessica, you're amazing," I said. "I just said those very words the other day—I need something to hold onto."

She looked up and smiled. "I know I may come across as a little out there, Nora. I can't help that; I'm an Aquarius," she said, as if that explained everything. "But I do know my stuff."

"I guess you do," I said, pulling myself back up to face the last card, the *Death* card. She was holding it in her hand now, as if she might get answers from it through osmosis.

"I believe you'll be leaving your job," she said with a sense of finality.

"That is the death?" I asked.

"Yes, I think as you deal with your fear of change, you will see that it is time to leave, that you've done all you could there."

"That I've helped as many people as I can?"

Jessica laughed. "Oh God, no," she said. "You're not there to help anyone else. You're there to help yourself."

"Help myself?"

"You have no idea how much you're learning there."

"You're right," I agreed. "I don't feel like I'm learning anything. I just feel tired most of the time."

"Oh, but Nora, this is one of those rare experiences," Jessica said. "This is one of those difficult experiences where you can't see it at the time, but twenty years from now you'll look back and not be able to believe all that you learned."

Quite frankly, I didn't believe her.

"You'll see," she said knowingly. And how could I argue with her? After everything else she'd said?

Jessica suddenly picked up the remaining deck and held it out to me.

"Here," she said. "Pick one more card, and we'll sum up your whole reading."

I let my fingers linger over the deck for a second, and then I just chose one randomly. She held it up for me. *The World.*

"Look at that," she said triumphantly. "Just as I was saying—the world is before you!"

Is that what she had been saying?

"You'll see what I mean," she said, knowing I wasn't getting it. "The world really is before you."

I would have to take her word for it.

Chapter Twenty

Maggie was sitting up in her wheelchair, her head tilted back as her mother leaned over her with tweezers.

"Hi, Nora," Maggie said, not moving her head.

"There we go," her mother said without turning to look at me. She moved the tweezers to Maggie's chin and pulled triumphantly.

I stared, a little horrified.

Maggie brought her head back to a normal angle, and her mother smiled at me as she took the tweezers back to the nightstand drawer.

"Do you know what the worst thing about aging is?" Maggie asked me.

"No," I said hesitantly.

"Chin hair," she said with disgust. "I just can't believe I have these little hairs sticking out of my chin. It makes me feel like Sister Mary Agnes."

Diane chuckled as she came back over by us. I was still just standing there, deeply distressed at the idea of growing chin hair someday.

Diane motioned to the chair next to Maggie. "Nora, have a seat," she said. "I'll pull a chair over from the other side of the room."

The curtain between the two beds was open today, but Diane paused as if she wanted to knock. She looked at Mrs. Lowry's bed, and I sensed she thought somehow she should ask permission.

"It's okay," I told her as I sat down. "I'll move it back when we're done. I think her daughter usually comes in the evenings."

"Yes," Maggie agreed. "Every Thursday evening."

Diane pulled the chair over. "Is that the only night she comes?" she asked.

Maggie shrugged. "There's not much she can do. She talks to her a little and strokes her hand. Usually she ends up making conversation with me. We'll usually watch *Mash* together while she's here. She said that was her mother's favorite show. I guess her mother really loved Klinger, so every time he comes on, she'll tell her mother he's on and what's happening. It's kind of sweet."

"Well, that's nice," Diane said absently. I could tell she was thinking about how the roles were reversed with her and Maggie. She frowned slightly.

"So you're back up, Maggie," I said, changing the subject.

"Yes," Maggie said, and she seemed happy about it, as if she had made her own choice this time. "And I'm painting." She nodded over towards the door.

"Painting?"

I turned and saw a canvas on an easel behind the door. I hadn't noticed it when I first came in. There just seemed to be blotches of color all over it.

"My mother suggested it," Maggie said.

"I thought it would be fun," Diane chimed in proudly.

"It is fun," Maggie admitted. "Of course, I can't hold the brush very well in my hand," she said, raising her crooked fingers, "thus the splotches. But I think it's a kind of modern style—impressionism or some such thing. Basically, just crap. But modern."

Diane laughed. I stood up and looked a little closer.

"It's kind of nice," I said, trying to sound enthusiastic.

"Don't humor me, Nora. It's crap, but it's fun. It's like art therapy, right Mom?"

"That's right," Diane agreed.

"I thought about holding the brush in my mouth, but that seemed a little dramatic," Maggie continued. "Although I may have had better results."

I sat back down.

"And I've been doing some writing," Maggie said, smiling at Diane. "My poor mother's been typing it all up for me since I really can't write with a pen anymore."

"I don't mind," Diane said.

I couldn't believe how well Maggie was doing. Jessica had been so right in her tarot card reading. Maggie was doing fine. Maybe there was just a period of adjustment she needed to go through, and now she could begin accepting this new lifestyle.

"There is one thing we need to talk about, though, Nora," Maggie said now, very seriously.

"Oh yeah, what's that?"

"You've never said what kind of Beatles girl you are."

I sighed. "Not that again," I said.

I looked from one to the other. They were both watching me expectantly.

"What about George? I'll say I'm a George girl."

Maggie scoffed.

"I can't be a George girl?" I asked, looking over at Diane who was also shaking her head.

"Why is it so hard for you to admit you're a John girl?" Maggie asked. "After all, I'm a John girl," she said proudly. She acted like I had just rejected her dog or her best friend or something.

"Oh, I don't know," I sighed. "I guess he just seems so airy fairy in a way."

"Airy fairy?" Maggie asked incredulously. "He is not airy fairy."

"Well, you know what I mean, all that singing about peace and love."

"He's an idealist," Diane said.

"Well, I can't be an idealist. I'm too much of a cynic."

"No, no," Maggie said, as if I just didn't understand anything. "Idealists are always cynics. It's because we expect too much of the world, and we're always disappointed."

I looked at her skeptically, like a cynic, I guess.

"I need someone to carry the mantle, and you're it," she said, shaking her head, as if this were not an option for me.

"Even if I don't want to?" I asked.

"You want to," she said. "Come on, it's not so hard to be an idealist. Give it a try."

"Okay, I guess I'm a John girl." What the hell? Would it kill me to be go along?

Maggie and Diane both cheered as if this were a huge moment. They certainly seemed to be enjoying this, even if I was annoyed by the whole thing.

"A John girl, it is," Maggie said, holding her plastic cup of water up as if to toast the occasion. Diane raised her water bottle. I held up my empty hands.

"That's okay, we got it," Maggie said, "clinking" with Diane and taking a really big, eager gulp.

I suddenly understood. "Maggie, that's not water, is it?"

"It's just a little vodka," she said. "I'm not driving."

"What about your medication?"

"It won't hurt anything."

I looked at Diane.

"I don't know what you're talking about," Diane said with mock innocence. I couldn't believe she was in on this.

"It's the middle of the afternoon," I protested.

"Oh, for God's sake, Nora, it's not like we have after-dinner drinks around here. I'm in bed by 8:00. Give me a break."

I was pretty sure this was against regulations, although I can't really say it had ever come up before. I looked at both of them. What could I do? Maggie took another sip, completely unconcerned that I would turn her in. She had such confidence in my inability to be a normal social worker.

"Well, I guess it's cocktail hour then," I said.

"There you go," Maggie said. I could see that she was relaxed, though not drunk. She seemed to read my thoughts.

"I'm just taking the edge off," she said. "I promise not to go speeding around the halls in my wheelchair and run anyone over."

"Yes, that might be a little difficult to explain."

"WWI—wheeling while intoxicated." Maggie enunciated the w's for effect, then chuckled and took another sip.

"So Maggie's sister is coming into town," Diane said suddenly.

I turned to look at her. "Really?" I was surprised.

"Yes, Liz is making a special trip," Maggie said. She sounded a little sarcastic, but I could tell she was pleased.

"And she's bringing the ukulele," Diane said.

"No shit?" Maggie said.

"The ukulele?" I asked.

They both started to laugh.

"It's a dumb family joke," Maggie said.

"It's from a camping trip we took a long time ago," Diane added.

"How long ago was that?" Maggie asked. "Let's see, I must have been about twelve, right?"

"I think so," Diane said. "Because I remember you were entering that bossy stage, and you were directing us all on how to pack the car and where everyone was expected to sit."

"I was not," Maggie laughed, but I sensed it was true.

"Yes, your father pulled me aside and asked, 'How long is this going to last?'"

Maggie laughed. "Little did he know it would last a lifetime."

"Maggie was the oldest," Diane said. "And I have to admit, she probably took on too much responsibility."

Maggie shrugged as she took another sip. I noticed she was really downing that drink.

"Maggie is quite a few years older than Liz, almost five years, and then Steve is only two years younger than Liz," Diane explained.

"Even Steve remembered the ukulele, and he was only five," Maggie said, finally setting her cup down on the wheeling table next to her. I still had no idea what the ukulele was all about, but they seemed in no hurry to explain it to me.

"And Maggie's father," Diane continued, "was well—" she hesitated.

"Working a lot," Maggie said. "Not really present, even when he was present, if you know what I mean."

I nodded.

"Yes, we struggled back then," Diane continued wistfully. "It was a difficult time in our family. And I think Maggie felt she had to take care of everything." It seemed as if Diane were trying to sum up Maggie's whole life, to explain why she ended up with this disease, as if her taking responsibility at a young age had somehow brought about this unfortunate sequence of events.

Maggie must have sensed this too. "Mom, it wasn't that bad. I was the oldest, after all. Isn't that what all oldest children do? Take on too much responsibility?"

"I suppose," Diane said thoughtfully.

"So what about the ukulele?" I asked.

"Well, we had this horrible trip," Maggie said with excitement, suddenly eager to explain it all.

"Maggie's father and I were arguing," Diane continued. "We had hit a rough spot in our marriage." I wanted to stop her and say, "Too much information." But finding out more than I ever wanted to know about people's lives was an occupational hazard. Luckily, she left it at that.

"The kids were fighting the whole way to the campgrounds," she was saying.

"Liz would not shut up about her doll she'd left at home," Maggie said with indignation, as if this had just happened yesterday.

"And Steve was whiny," Diane continued.

"Steve was always whiny," Maggie added.

"So we got to the campgrounds," Diane went on, "and it was raining. I mean, really raining. And we couldn't get the tent up."

"Even with my expert directions," Maggie said.

"Yes, well it was a new tent, still in the box, and Maggie felt the need to read the directions on setting up the tent to her father," Diane said, "which annoyed him to no end."

"My dad was the kind of guy who thought he could do everything." Maggie hesitated. "Maybe they're all like that," she said suddenly, chuckling to herself. "But at twelve, I didn't know what an insult it was for me to try to tell him how to set up the tent."

"Oh, and the bread was soggy and Liz dumped the cooler out of the back of the station wagon," Diane said. "It just went on and on. I think you get the picture."

"I do," I said.

"So finally, we were able to get up the tent, and eat some dinner, and that evening the weather cleared," Diane told me.

"Finally," Maggie added. "You would not believe how much it rained that day. I still feel soaked to the bone just thinking about it." She shivered.

"There was a communal area on the campgrounds with a big fire pit," Diane went on, "and there were several other campers, mostly families, sitting around it, roasting marshmallows, drinking beer and pop, that sort of thing. So we went out to join them."

"And then came the guy with the ukulele," Maggie said.

"We were really tired," Diane added. "It had been such a long day. Maybe we were a little punchy."

"I don't think that was it," Maggie said.

"What do you mean?" I asked.

"This guy started playing his ukulele and it was the most god-awful sound you'd ever heard," Maggie said.

"Just terrible," Diane agreed.

"We don't even know where he came from," Maggie said. "He didn't seem to be with any of the other families or know anyone else there. But he came and sat down and suddenly pulled out his ukulele. He started strumming a few awful notes and trying to sing. We think he was playing 'House of the Rising Sun,' but we were never quite sure. He kept getting the words wrong, and he'd confuse it with that other song. What was it, Mom?"

"The Arlo Guthrie song about New Orleans. He had the words so mixed up. Something like, 'There is a house in New Orleans that's been gone five hundred years.' Was that it?" she asked Maggie.

Maggie was laughing now and shook her head. "I don't know," she said.

"It was the craziest thing you'd ever heard," Diane said. They were both laughing now.

"And we couldn't help it," Maggie said. "We were just cracking up and trying not to show it."

They were both becoming breathless as they told the story, laughing harder as they went on.

"Even your father couldn't control himself," Diane said, wiping her eyes. "He told me later that the sound of that droning from the ukulele just set him off and there was no turning back."

"And then remember Steve said, 'Mom, is that guitar sick?'" Maggie was doubling over in her wheelchair, she was laughing so hard.

"Oh, that was it for me," Diane said. "I couldn't even breathe after that."

Maggie could hardly get her sentences out now. "But you said, 'No honey, it's just a little guitar.'"

Diane started to lean forward in her chair too, trying to catch her breath. I had to laugh just watching them. It was one of those stories where the people are really telling it for themselves and only need an audience as an excuse to tell it one more time.

They both straightened up now and Diane went over and got some tissue. She handed some to Maggie. They both began wiping their eyes.

"So, anyway," Maggie said. "The next morning when Liz got up to go to the bathroom—she always had to go to the bathroom," she added as a sidebar, "she found the ukulele sitting there by the campfire."

"We looked around for the man and couldn't find him," Diane said as if she still couldn't believe it. "He had just left it there."

"Maybe we helped him realize he really couldn't play it," Maggie said.

"I think he was an angel who showed up at just the right time," Diane said suddenly.

"Mom!" Maggie stared at her mother. She'd apparently never heard this theory before. "That's a little ridiculous."

"Well, it is possible, you know, that angels sometimes show up in different forms," Diane said, a little defensively.

"As a bad ukulele player?" Maggie asked incredulously.

"I'm just saying that our trip really improved after that. A lot of things in the family improved after that, you have to admit. It was as if we'd reached some kind of breaking point, and that man just kind of nudged us towards a better place."

Maggie turned to me. "I'm the only normal one in the family," she said, shaking her head and taking another sip of her drink, as if that were the only thing that got her through this craziness.

I smiled. "So Liz has the ukulele now?" I asked.

"Well, what happened," Diane said, "is that we kept the ukulele in our family room for years after that. It was really like a family treasure." She looked at Maggie as if to say that this proved her whole point. "And then as the kids grew up and moved out, each of them wanted to take it with them. We decided to pass it around. Everyone got a chance to keep it for a while and was expected to bring it to the next family gathering and pass it on to the next person."

"When did we stop doing that?" Maggie asked Diane. "When Dad died?"

"No," Diane said quietly. "I think it was when you got sick."

"Oh," Maggie said. They were both silent for a minute. I didn't say anything. I wasn't sure what was going on.

"Liz will have a hard time seeing me here," Maggie said finally.

"Yes," Diane agreed. "Yes, she will. But she's trying."

Maggie nodded and looked at me. "With my being the oldest and so bossy—" She stopped and smiled slightly. "It's been hard for them to get used to my—" She waved her hand as if trying to find the right word. "I guess my helplessness. They don't know what to do with it."

Diane nodded. "But they're trying," she said again. I realized how annoying that must be—to constantly hear how much everyone was trying to deal with something you had no choice but to deal with.

"So, I get the ukulele now," Maggie said, looking around the room as if she were trying to figure out how it would fit in with the décor.

"Maybe on the nightstand," Diane said. Maggie nodded and then shrugged. There would be plenty of time for redecorating.

"You know," she said suddenly, "my favorite childhood memory is of a horrible ukulele player who my mother thinks was an angel sent to save our family from despair." Maggie and I looked at each other and began to laugh.

Diane shook her head. "It's not as far-fetched as it sounds."

I stayed for a while longer, listening to some more family stories and then left them to their own vodka party. I smiled when I left Maggie's room that day. It was one of the most satisfying moments of my career as a social worker. It seemed we had come such a long way. Maggie was finally coming to terms with the MS, and maybe, you could say, so was I. As Jessica had said, we were both on our own journeys, going about things in our own way. But at least I knew now that Maggie was going to be alright. And maybe I was going to be alright too.

Chapter Twenty-One

I knew something was up as soon as I walked in my office and saw Cathy and Allison waiting for me.

"What's going on?"

"Why don't you sit down, Nora?" Cathy said.

That was never a good start to a conversation. I sat down.

"It's Maggie," Allison said.

"Is she depressed again?"

They glanced at each other.

"What?" I asked.

"She's gone."

"Gone? Like she checked out?"

"She had a heart attack and died in her sleep last night," Cathy said. Allison looked away.

I stared at Cathy. I heard the words, but my mind could not understand them.

"Wait—what?"

"She died last night, Nora."

I kept staring at them.

"That's not possible. She was fine. I just saw her the other day. She was fine."

They didn't say anything. Allison kept looking away. I thought maybe she was crying. Cathy had that kind of strange, sappy look on her face that people get when they really do feel for you but are trying too hard to show it. That's how I knew this was real. I could see that Cathy felt really sorry for me, and I couldn't stand it.

"People with MS don't die of heart attacks," I said. I kept feeling like I had to talk them out of it, that if I could find an explanation that made sense, they would be wrong.

"Anyone can die of a heart attack," Allison said, turning towards me. I could see that tears were streaming down her face.

"It wasn't the MS," Cathy said in a very official nurse's voice. "But it could have been the stress of having a major disease, of moving here, her marriage ending. Any number of stressors could have triggered this. I believe her father died of heart disease at a fairly young age."

I just kept staring at Cathy. This couldn't be possible. How could someone have such a horrible disease and then die of another horrible disease? How could Maggie be gone?

"Jessica said she would be fine," I said suddenly.

"Who's Jessica?" Allison asked.

But I couldn't answer. The room was spinning around, and I suddenly felt sick to my stomach. Being nurses, they both must have noticed this at the same time.

"Put your head between your knees," Cathy ordered, coming towards me and putting her hand on my back as I leaned forward.

"I'll get some water," I heard Allison say, and her footsteps tapped out into the hallway.

"It's okay, Nora. Try to keep breathing evenly."

"This just doesn't make any sense," I mumbled from my position. I stared at the floor, trying to will it to stop spinning. Finally, I closed my eyes.

"It's unusual," I heard Cathy say as Allison's footsteps came back into the room. "No one expected this. But the heart is a funny thing."

I wanted to laugh. It sounded like she was talking about love, not death.

"Do you want to try to sit up?" Cathy asked, and I brought my head up gingerly.

Allison handed me the water. "Just take small sips," she said.

I tried. I took one small sip and then I leaned over, grabbed the trash can from under my desk, and puked right into it.

It was decided then that I needed to go home. I wasn't involved in the planning. I sat at my desk with my head in my hands while Allison somehow figured out how to call Sharon. Maybe I gave her the number? I can't remember. They all decided that Sharon would come and pick me up and Allison would get her boyfriend to follow her after work while she drove my car back to my place. At least that's what happened, so I guess that's what they all figured out.

Several other nurses came and went as I sat there.

"Do you think she's in shock?" I heard one of them ask. I'm not sure what the answer was, but no one suggested I go to the hospital, so I guess it was no. Later, when I thought back on it all, I realized how strange it was that I was like one of the patients that day. For months, I had watched all of the nurses treat the residents in the nursing home with so much care and concern, and here I was the recipient of that same treatment. If ever I had lost all semblance of professionalism, it was that day. But at the time, I didn't even notice. I couldn't process anything that was happening.

Sharon arrived and I went with her to her car. Allison and Cathy came out with us and helped "tuck me" into the front seat. At least, that's what it felt like.

"Everyone's being so nice," I remember saying as Sharon started the car. I don't remember what she answered.

She took me back to my apartment. Barney Fife was so thrilled to see me. He thought it was a special treat that I was home so soon after I'd left for the day. But even he seemed to notice my state of mind. He settled down quietly next to me as I sat on the couch.

I remember Sharon offering me things—soup, ginger ale, ibuprofen. It was as if I were sick. She kept apologizing for having to go back to work, but she couldn't miss any more time. Her boss had let her leave as a special favor.

I waved her away. "I'm fine," I lied. But I wanted to be alone anyway.

Barney and I sat on the couch for a long time. I remember thinking that I'd never stayed in one place in my apartment for so long. I watched as the sun progressed from the kitchen window in the back of the apartment to the dining room and into the front living room where we sat. By the time it made it to the big front window, the light was shining right into my eyes, but still I didn't change my position. If I moved, I would feel, and that was the one thing I didn't want to do. I just wanted to stop life from going forward; I wanted to just stay in this position forever so that nothing bad could ever happen again. I could hear the answering machine going off in the background—Sharon calling from work, Allison, then Cathy, from the nursing home. I didn't answer any of them.

The thing that finally got me was I had to go to the bathroom. I couldn't hold it anymore. I shifted and Barney looked up at me expectantly. It was as if he weren't sure I was still alive. Just as I knew they would, the tears started as soon as I moved. I had to go so bad I ran to the bathroom, and the whole time I felt tears just streaming down my face. I grabbed extra toilet paper as I sat on the toilet, fluid coming out of me from both ends, and I sobbed into it as I peed.

When I came back to the living room, Barney was sitting up on the couch. I knew he wanted to go for a walk, but I sat down next to him and buried my face in his fur. All I could think about was Maggie's awful painting. She would never get to finish it. She would never get to see her sister who was making a special trip with the ukulele. There would be no need to find the right place for the ukulele in her room. I would never again get to talk to her about life, about all those things that didn't seem to matter to anyone else, but that we could talk about for hours. I cried for the longest time.

Barney had to wait until late for his walk. Allison arrived with the car and came into check on me. Sharon left another message on my answering machine and demanded that I call her back. Then she brought me soup and ginger ale after work. It was all she knew to do, she said. The ginger ale was a good idea, actually, since I couldn't get over the feeling of being nauseous all day.

Finally, Barney and I went for a long walk. He was delighted to run into his Rottweiler friend, and I made small talk with the owner while they played. Luckily, it was too dark for him to see my puffy eyes and blotchy face, so he didn't even notice anything was wrong. Finally, I called for Barney, and we walked slowly home. Barney seemed to match my mood, barely noticing the smells along the way.

When we got back to the apartment, I sat back down on the couch. There was no more sunlight to watch making its way across the apartment. I couldn't bear to turn on the TV and listen to mindless chatter. I just sat staring at the wall in the dark.

Finally, I picked up the phone.

It rang four times, and I was about to hang up before the voicemail kicked in, but she picked it up at the last minute.

"Mom?"

"Nora," she said enthusiastically. Then it seemed to hit her that I never called. "What's wrong?"

"I'm fine," I said, knowing that's what she was thinking. But my voice was shaky.

"What happened?"

"One of the patients at the nursing home died today," I said.

There was a pause on the other end of the phone. "And this is unusual?" she asked, sounding genuinely confused.

I sighed. Did I really want to go into it all? Did I want to hear the reasons why this really shouldn't matter so much to me? Did I want to try to explain MS and how sick it made her, and yet somehow she didn't even die from that? Did I want to hear about why I needed to find a different job?

"She was a younger patient, someone I kind of got to know pretty well," I said as simply as I could. "I didn't know her that long, but—" I could hear my voice breaking and I stopped.

"Hold on a minute, Nora," my mother said suddenly. I sighed again. Leave it to my mother to ask me to hang on the line in the middle of an emotional crisis. She was gone for a few minutes while I debated whether to hang up or not. But finally, she came back.

"Are you ready for bed?" she asked as if I were twelve years old. I looked at myself in my old t-shirt and sweats.

"I guess so," I said. "Why?"

"Go climb into bed and get comfortable," she said in a conspiratorial tone. "But take the phone with you." In a better moment, I would have had a smart remark about how I wouldn't still be able to hear her if I didn't take the phone, but I was too tired.

I settled myself into bed and Barney Fife jumped up next to me. He lay with his head between his paws expectantly.

"Okay," she said. "Are you ready?"

"Yes."

"Do you remember the story about Maureen?" she asked.

Maureen. I hadn't thought of it in years. When I was about six, not long after my father left, I'd decided I didn't like the name Nora, and I kept asking my mother why she had named me that. "Why couldn't you have named me something nice, like Maureen?" I asked. I think it was just my wanting to blame my mother for something, and not naming me Maureen seemed like the best idea at the time.

So my mother listened to this over and over. Then one night when she was getting ready to read me a story, and I was telling her how much better my life would be if my name were Maureen, she said, "You know what? I have a story about Maureen." She made up a story about Maureen right on the spot. And from then on, for about six months, that was the only story I wanted to hear. I was living vicariously through Maureen, which was the name I felt I should have had anyway.

She started the story now as I listened on the phone. "Maureen always loved to watch the moon from her window." I could tell she was reading.

"You wrote it down?" I asked, surprised.

"Of course. Did you think I could remember all of it?"

"I don't remember you reading it back then."

"No, I kept a copy in the drawer in case I forgot anything. I don't know why I bothered. You never even noticed that the details would change when I forgot something."

No, I hadn't noticed that. And here I'd thought I was such a sharp six-year-old.

She went on. "Maureen wanted to go to the moon someday, but she was told she had to be very smart for that, even smarter than the men who were able to go."

I was surprised now by my mother's feminist slant. I hadn't realized she had it in her.

"Maureen loved the way the moon changed shapes over time. Sometimes it was full, sometimes it was slanted, and sometimes it had a big smile in it."

I settled back on my pillow. I'd never realized what a really dumb story this was. But I felt my eyes closing in spite of myself.

"Maureen wished every night on that moon, that one day she would go there."

I could feel myself starting to doze off as she read. I'm not sure if it was because the story was so soothing or because it was so boring. But as I lay there half-asleep, I was suddenly touched that my mother had made up a story just for me, and that she had used the name I complained she didn't give me.

"I don't remember how it ends," I mumbled into the phone.

"Oh, she goes to the moon," I heard her say with conviction. "Of course she does."

It was something only a mother could be so sure about, I thought as I drifted off to sleep.

Chapter Twenty-Two

Allison and I went to Maggie's funeral together. Since it wasn't really standard protocol for us to attend our patients' funerals, we stayed in the back, not wanting to intrude on the family and friends. I was surprised at how many people were there. I had seen none of them except Diane at the nursing home.

I was also surprised to find out it was a Catholic funeral. I remembered that Maggie had said her parents were Catholics, but she had obviously not been a practicing one before she died. It was a very old-fashioned kind of church with statues and pews, and tall—very tall—ceilings. I looked up at the rafters and wondered if there could be a bird's nest hidden in there. It would suit Maggie's funeral if a bird would swoop down in the middle of it and make a commotion, but I didn't think it was possible. The church looked too clean and well-cared for to be hiding any bird's nests in its beams.

The service began very solemnly with the family walking in behind the coffin and the priest just ahead, waving some kind of strange looking can thing that was obviously incense. The smell was overwhelming. Allison started to gag as he went right by her on the aisle, and I had to hand her a tissue from my purse to cough into. Not exactly the best way to stay inconspicuous.

I watched the family closely as they followed the coffin. Holding Diane's arm on one side was obviously Maggie's sister Liz, as she looked like a much younger version of Maggie with long, flowing dark hair and a less tired looking face. On the other side of Diane was Maggie's brother Steve, I was sure, as he too carried a family resemblance, though not as distinct. Directly behind them were a few children, the nieces and nephews, and guiding the children from behind were another man and woman who I was pretty sure were Liz and Steve's respective spouses, as they looked lost and a little out of place.

The family walked slowly as organ music played softly in the background. The only other sounds you could hear were some quiet sniffling noises and rustling as people reached for their tissue. Diane smiled at some of the people she passed and even reached her hand out to someone as they neared the front. I was surprised at her calm, magnanimous gestures, though I'm not sure why. She had been that way all along. When they reached the first row, Diane stopped and hugged a man in the pew directly behind them, and I wondered if that was Maggie's soon-to-be ex-husband.

Allison was thinking the same thing. She leaned over and whispered, "The ex?"

I shrugged. But it had to be. He was nothing like someone I would picture Maggie with. He was tall and lanky with blond hair that seemed to be thinning. He seemed very serious, although to cut him some slack, he was at a funeral, but still, there was just an air about him that was so dull, so staid maybe, and I couldn't picture him laughing at any of Maggie's jokes. I couldn't even picture him knowing that she was telling a joke. But then again, how could I know all that just from looking at the guy? Maybe I just wanted to justify Maggie's saying she never loved him.

What an awkward situation, I thought, the divorce not even final yet, Maggie dying in the nursing home before they even had a chance to make it official. What was the family to do? Not include him in the service? Make him sit in the back? And how unfortunate for him, having to play the schmuck who divorced his disabled wife as she goes into a nursing home, and then, to make it even worse, she goes and dies on him before the paperwork is completed. I was thinking how much Maggie would appreciate the drama of it all, the whole tabloid feel to it.

I wasn't sure she would appreciate the service, though, I realized as it went on, as I sat and then stood, and then kneeled, and then stood, and then sat. It was confusing and exhausting, and I couldn't even imagine Maggie wanting this kind of ceremony. There were lots of prayers and bible readings, and then finally the priest stood to talk.

He was an older man who seemed to have some trouble remembering details, and it was obvious from his comments that he didn't even know Maggie. He talked about her in very general terms, what a wonderful daughter, sister, wife she had been. Allison and I both cringed at the wife part, though I wasn't sure anyone else around us did. I wondered if everyone knew about the divorce. At another point, the priest called her "Mary." This time a collective cringe went through the crowd. Finally, he stopped speaking and I was relieved to hear him offer some time for others to come up and share memories of Maggie.

Liz stood up and then Steve. They talked about a Maggie I didn't really know, the "bossy older sister" who nevertheless always stood up for them and made sure they stayed out of trouble. Steve told a story about the time Maggie was driving all of them to school and accidentally backed into a fire hydrant and set it off and how they all arrived at school soaking wet. Steve and Liz were forbidden to tell on her so that she wouldn't lose her driving privileges, but unfortunately the large dent in the bumper gave her away, not to mention that the school called their parents when they arrived soaked to the bone. Everyone laughed appreciatively at that.

A friend from high school stood up and talked about the girls' basketball team and the fun times they had. Another friend from college, and then one she knew later, also shared stories about Maggie, and the very ordinary things they had done together. I remembered how Maggie had described herself that way—ordinary. It was one of the things I think she regretted most about her life.

It was only Diane who spoke about Maggie's illness. She was the last one to go up to the lectern, and as she talked, there was a slight rustling in the crowd, an unease, almost a sense that no one wanted to admit the obvious—Maggie had died in a nursing home. Diane talked about it gently, though, not wanting to offend anyone, not wanting to force-feed the uncomfortable truth to the family and friends who were there to remember the old Maggie, the one she had been before she became so sick. She spoke briefly about Maggie's struggles with her weakening body, her reluctance to go to the nursing home, her refusal to put the burden on anyone else, and finally her courage in facing the inevitable.

It's right out of *Brian's Song,* I said to Maggie in my head, and then I caught myself, surprised to find myself talking to her as if she were still here.

I made it through the service, even Diane's heartfelt tribute, without a tear. I wanted to maintain my composure, and I noticed Allison doing the same. I think we were trying to represent the nursing home as professionals, though no one had asked us to do that. It was something we took upon ourselves.

But then something totally unexpected happened. At the end of the service, a young woman stood up with her guitar. The organ was silenced. The incense was put away. The prayers were over. She strummed slowly on the guitar, and then began softly singing "Imagine." That was the end of my composure, as well as Allison's. I kept feeding tissues to her as the two of us sat in the back row, professional representatives of Longate Nursing Home, sobbing. I think we finally felt like we were at Maggie's funeral.

Afterwards, there was a small reception in a hall next to the church. The family was mingling with the funeral attendees. Allison began a conversation with Liz, while I went up to Diane.

"Nora," Diane said, taking my hand. "I'm so glad you came."

"Of course. I wouldn't miss it," I said, looking around the church hall as if I weren't sure where I was.

Diane seemed to know exactly what I was thinking. "I know, it's not really Maggie. But she wanted it to be a Catholic funeral. Her father was a staunch Catholic, and Maggie wanted to do it out of respect for him."

"Really?" I asked, surprised at the gesture.

"Maggie adored her father," Diane said quietly. "She didn't talk about him much so you might not have known that. But she was really devastated when he died."

"No, I didn't know that," I said, feeling like there was so much I didn't know. But it made sense that Maggie wouldn't really care so much about her funeral or what the service was like. It might as well have been Catholic to please her father.

"Listen, Nora," Diane said now, reaching over to the table behind her and pulling an envelope from her purse. "I have a letter for you."

"A letter?" I asked, confused.

"Yes, from Maggie."

"She wrote me a letter?"

"She wrote them for a lot of people," Diane said. "That was the writing she said she was doing, and I was typing them up for her." She handed me the envelope. "They were her last letters, I guess."

"So she told you she thought she was going to die?" I asked before I realized how blunt that sounded.

Diane shrugged. "Not in so many words. Her letters hint at it, of course." She laughed now, a little sadly. "She knew so well how to work me. She told me it was therapy, just a way for her to get out all her pent-up feelings about the changes in her life. She knew I'd go along with anything I thought was therapy."

I smiled. That sounded like Maggie.

"Well, I guess I feel honored that I got one."

"Oh, she appreciated you, kiddo," Diane said and suddenly reached out and hugged me. "You were there to listen to her at the end when even I couldn't listen sometimes." Her eyes were filled with tears as she released me.

"She understood that," I said, though I had no idea if she really did. There was really so much I never knew about Maggie, and now I never would.

Diane nodded, and someone else came up to her then to offer condolences. I waved a slight goodbye, and Diane smiled and turned to the next person.

Allison found me and we decided to go. "Poor Liz," she said as we walked out. "She feels so bad that she didn't make it before Maggie died."

"Yes, that was sad," I agreed absently as we left. I wondered how many people Maggie had left letters for. I hoped she had thought to leave one for Liz.

I put the letter in my desk at work for the rest of the day. When I went home, I was busy taking care of Barney and finding things to do around the apartment. I think I was afraid to read it. I had no idea what Maggie would say to me. And it was creepy somehow to read the words of someone who was no longer here. It was like she was speaking to me from the grave.

Finally late that night, I opened the envelope.

Dear Nora,

As you know from our many conversations, I've had way too much time on my hands lately. Time to contemplate the secrets of the universe, which is something I've never really tried to do before. I still haven't got it all figured out, but I can't tell you how much I appreciate your taking the time to listen to my ramblings. And all without medication! (For either of us.)

You didn't tell me this, but I know it's important to you for everything in life to make sense. It drives you crazy when the world seems meaningless. I know this because I'm the same way. So here's some meaning for you—what I've realized is that this crazy disease, which seems so cruel and cold, has actually taught me how to feel again. Who knew it could do something like that? I was so angry that everything seemed to be taken away from me, but what I've realized as I've felt all of this anger and grief and pain is that I hadn't been feeling much at all in my life before. I was just going through the motions, living the life I thought I was expected to live. I'm not even sure there was anything to be taken away from me. Remember when I told you I stayed busy so I wouldn't have to feel the fear of having MS? The truth is I stayed busy so I wouldn't have to feel anything.

What I want to make sure I tell you, because I'm sure no one else will, is to keep feeling everything around you. I can see that you do, that you haven't yet lost your capacity to feel. People will try to tell you that you're crazy and wrong for feeling things. They will try to talk you into not expressing any of it. Don't let them! And most of all, don't talk yourself into leading a life just like everyone else's

So, my fellow John girl, it's up to you to carry on! Imagine that.

Love always,
Maggie

I sat staring at the letter for a long time after I read it. I'm not sure what I was expecting—a *Brian's Song* moment? Reasons why I should help MS patients? Her theories on life after death? But what I was not expecting was what I got. I wasn't quite sure what to do with it.

Finally, I did the only thing I could think of. I went to my computer and Googled the lyrics to "Imagine."

Chapter Twenty-Three

In the few weeks after Maggie's death, it was like falling into a dark hole with no way out. I couldn't find my way back to normal. People at work were concerned. They were very nice to me, almost apologetic if they had to ask me to do my job, which I wasn't doing very well. I stayed locked in my office much of the time, working on the piles of paperwork I always had to do anyway. I knew I should be doing more than that; I should be visiting the other patients. But I couldn't bring myself to walk by Maggie's room. It didn't stay empty for long. Within days, the bed was filled by an eighty-year-old woman who could no longer stay in assisted living. The administrator of the nursing home was nice enough to take the social history on the woman, but I knew one day I would have to go in there to visit her and face the empty white wall without John Lennon staring at me.

At home, I stayed in almost all of the time, except to walk Barney Fife. Sharon kept asking me to do things. A few people from the church called to check in. My mother called more often, but I just kept telling her everything was fine. I'm sure she could sense it wasn't.

I could see exactly what Maggie had been saying. They all wanted to talk me out of my grief. They wanted me to stop being depressed and get back to living, though what kind of living can there be if you can't take a few weeks to be sad about your friend dying?

Then one night I had a dream.

I was sitting in Maggie's wheelchair in her room at the nursing home, and Maggie came walking in the door. She was dressed in a bright red satin top with nice jeans and boots. Her wavy hair had no gray and her face was all done up, almost like she'd had a make-over. I realized I'd never seen her any other way than in jeans and a t-shirt or pajamas. She looked incredible.

"Hi, Nora," she said. "I want you to see something."

She suddenly began spinning in circles. All of her limbs were working perfectly as she went round and round until I was dizzy just from watching her.

"Remember when you were a little kid," she called out to me as she circled around, "and you could just keep spinning and spinning and never get dizzy?" She came to a sudden stop. "I can do that again. It's so cool."

I just stared at her, and finally she came over and sat in the chair in front of me.

"Nora, what are you doing in that wheelchair?" she asked.

"I don't know."

"Well, let me tell you," she said. "You're sad that I'm gone. But even more so, you're sad that life is so hard, that just when you think everything is starting to make sense, it whacks you over the head and you just don't even know how to cope with that."

"Yes," I agreed.

"And you feel like it's all useless, like what's the point? Here you are trying to help people, trying to make a difference, but it all seems like a waste of time."

"Are you inside my head?" I asked, a little alarmed.

"Of course I am. You're dreaming, remember?"

I stared at her, confused. Was I dreaming or was this real?

Maggie just laughed. "I don't need to be inside your head. You're emanating that energy all over the place right now. I couldn't miss it if I tried."

"Oh," I said, a little relieved. She waited for me to say something.

"The tarot card reader said you were going to be fine." My voice sounded like I was pouting, as if I were five years old and didn't get the toy I wanted for Christmas.

"I am fine," she said.

"But she said you were beginning a new journey," I protested.

"I am beginning a new journey."

I paused, trying to understand.

"So this is what she meant?"

"She didn't know what she meant," Maggie said. "She was just reading the energy."

I sighed. "I don't get why you died. You didn't get to do any of the things you wanted. I mean, maybe you could have been healed or something." I knew this all sounded so feeble, but I couldn't stand the fact that it had all worked out this way.

"Nora," Maggie said gently, "I was done with my life. I did get to do the things I wanted. I fell in love, I was in a great play, I had a wonderful relationship with my parents, and even my brother and sister. I had friends who I had so much fun with."

"And that's it?" I asked, so disappointed. "What about your dreams? What about what you said about just going through the motions?"

"Yes," she said. "And I learned something so valuable in my life. I learned how important it is to really feel and experience your life. Do you know that people can do all the things I wanted to do—go to Paris and travel around the world and ride a motorcycle across country—but never really experience it? It's not about what you do; it's about how you do it. You have to live from your soul and not just on the surface. I learned that."

"You went through all of that suffering just to learn *that*?"

"But how important is that? It's everything. So yes, in a way you could say I sacrificed my life for my soul. But after all, what is life without your soul? But I don't really see it as a sacrifice anymore. I see it as so much more than that. It was a rare experience. I can't believe all I learned from it."

Why did that sound so familiar? Where had I heard that before?

"So what will you do now?" I asked.

"Well, I'll go to Paris, and I'll ride across the country on a motorcycle, and I'll paint and I'll act in great plays, and I'll sing—"

"You're really going to do all that now?"

"Not exactly," she said. "It's the essence of those things I was looking for. It's the freedom and the joy I was looking for, not those actual things." She paused. "It's so hard for you to understand when you're still human, Nora. It's never going to make complete sense to you in your lifetime, no matter how hard you try to work it all out in your head. The only real answers you're going to get are through your experiences."

I sighed. "That's not what I want to hear."

Maggie laughed. "I know, you want something you can hold onto."

"I want something more than this." I motioned around me at the sterile nursing home room.

"But there is so much more," she said. "There are so many experiences. It's like when you go to a movie, you don't want to go to the same one all

148

the time. So sometimes you go to a comedy, other times you go to a tear-jerker. Once in a while, you even go to a horror flick, and then you regret it when you're lying in your bed with a knife under your pillow. But it's still so much fun? You see? "

"I don't know."

"There is so much to experience," she repeated. "On your side and mine."

I thought about that for a minute, not sure what to make of it.

"Will I ever see you again?"

"Of course," Maggie said simply. "We've been friends for a very long time."

I nodded as if I knew what she was saying were true, but I didn't know how I knew it.

"Listen, Nora, will you do me a favor?"

"What?"

"Will you talk to my mom? You know, it's strange. For all her mysticism, she is really hard to get through to."

"I would have thought that someone who believes angels show up playing ukuleles would be easy to reach."

Maggie chuckled. "Yeah, I thought the same thing, but no go. Anyway, can you tell her that my dad understands all about Joe now?"

"Oh God," I said, holding up my hand in protest. "I don't want to get in the middle of your parents' marriage."

Maggie laughed. "Oh, for God's sake, Nora, Joe was the cat."

"The cat?"

"Yes, it was my father's cat. Right before he died, my mother accidentally let the cat out and he was hit by a car. My father was furious with her, and then before they ever had a chance to work it out, my father suddenly died. It's weighed on my mother all these years."

"The cat?" I asked again. This was the profound message I was to deliver from beyond? Well, I guess if something like that had happened to Barney Fife, I would want to know too.

"It will mean so much to her. Tell her Joe is with my dad. He wanted to go with my dad, and that's why it happened the way it did."

"Of course," I said. "I'll tell her. But don't you want me to let her know you're okay? Or that your father's okay?"

"Oh, she already knows that," Maggie said simply.

We sat quietly for a minute. Then Maggie suddenly stood up and motioned for me to get out of the wheelchair.

"Come on, Nora, let's go," was all she said. And we walked out of the room together.

I woke up with a start, not sure where I was for a minute. I was surprised to find myself staring at the ceiling of my bedroom. I heard Barney Fife next to me, and I looked over at him. He was sitting up, wide awake. His ears were perked, his head was slightly cocked, and his tail was wagging. He was staring at the door to my room.

Chapter Twenty-Four

*M*r. Gordon waved me into his room as I passed.

"Hello, Mr. Gordon," I said. "I can't stay. I'm just about to—" I stopped as I saw what he was holding up. It was a shiny paperback book with black and brown trim and in bold print the title: *The Twentieth Century War.*

"You were published," I said in shock.

"Self-published," he corrected me.

"Really?"

He handed me the book, and I turned it over to look at the back cover and then flipped through the pages. It looked so professional.

"Yes, that young nurse's aide helped me. What's her name?" I couldn't be sure which one he meant.

"You know, long brown hair, pretty girl, always taking my temperature."

"Allison?" I asked.

"Yes, that's her name."

"Allison is a nurse, Mr. Gordon, not an aide."

"Pfft," he said, waving his hand to dismiss me. "She can't be a nurse. She's not even out of high school."

I smiled. I couldn't help but be pleased that Allison too was perceived by Mr. Gordon as too young to do anything important.

"So she helped you get this published?"

"Yes," he said proudly. "She went on that Intronet and for a nominal fee of $2,000 was able to get my book published. Isn't it wonderful?"

I couldn't figure out how anyone could find $2,000 a nominal fee, but I agreed that yes, it was wonderful. I went to hand the book back to Mr. Gordon.

"No, no," he said, pushing it back. He opened the front cover as he was giving it to me, and I saw that he had signed it: *To Nora, my favorite Activity Director—Charles Gordon.*

"It's yours to keep," he said. "Read and enjoy."

"Thank you, Mr. Gordon. " I was almost entirely sure that I wouldn't enjoy it, but I smiled politely. He smiled back at me with an obvious sense of pride. I carried the book out of his room, still marveling that it had really been published.

Allison was waiting in the lobby for me with Mrs. Wellington. I held the book up as I approached. "We have a published author in our nursing home."

Allison smiled proudly, as if it were one of her children I was talking about.

"That was such a good idea," I told her.

She shrugged. "Well, I hated to see all that time and effort he put into it go to waste."

Mrs. Wellington cleared her throat loudly to remind us that she was the one we should be paying attention to right now.

"I have all the exit paperwork over her, Mrs. Wellington," I said, going over to the front desk where the receptionist was holding it for me and bringing it back with me. I leaned down and picked up her suitcase, and Allison began slowly pushing the wheelchair out the front door. I was reading from the papers in my hand as we walked.

"So the home health aide will be able to get you breakfast when she comes in the morning, and Meals on Wheels will bring a hot lunch and make sure you have what you need for dinner."

I went on—the scheduled doctors' appointments, the neighbor who said she'd check in on her, everything Mrs. Wellington would possibly need to know for her return home after what we liked to think of as her rehabilitative stay at the nursing home. I'm sure she had other ways of putting it.

The cab was waiting by the curb. Allison pushed the wheelchair over next to it and adjusted the chair so that it was in position next to the cab's door.

"So you should be all set," I said, handing Mrs. Wellington the papers. She took them demurely. She was especially subdued this morning.

"Thank you, dear," she said sweetly. I glanced at Allison who was still behind the wheelchair. She shrugged.

The cab driver came around and took the suitcase from me. He opened up the trunk and put it in. I held the wheelchair in place while Allison helped Mrs. Wellington out of it and into the back of the cab.

"Are you comfortable?" Allison asked her as she settled her in.

"I'm fine," Mrs. Wellington said. "Thank you, dear."

The cab driver pushed the wheelchair arms together and lifted it into the trunk. There were some loud banging noises that shook the vehicle as he maneuvered the suitcase and somehow managed to squeeze it all in.

Allison leaned back and was ready to shut the door.

"The aide will be there to help you into your house when you get home," I told Mrs. Wellington from behind Allison. "You call if you need anything."

"Goodbye, Mrs. Wellington," Allison said as she closed the door.

I gave the cab driver a piece of paper with Mrs. Wellington's address on it, and then he went around and got into the driver's seat.

Allison and I stood waving on the curb as the cab pulled away. It made it about fifty feet and then suddenly came to a stop again. We could see the back window rolling ever so slowly down. It seemed to take forever and then finally, bit by bit, Mrs. Wellington's head came out.

Allison and I leaned forward in anticipation.

Mrs. Wellington's voice cracked as she spoke. "I am never coming back to this shit-ass nursing home," she said matter-of-factly. Then her head moved just as slowly back inside the cab, the window began its long roll up, and the cab pulled away from the curb again.

Allison and I both kept leaning forward, our hands still raised as if we wanted to wave, but neither of us did. It took us a couple of seconds, and then Allison began to lean back and I followed. We put our hands down. There was silence.

"Well, that was a heart-warming moment," I said finally.

"Yes," Allison agreed, putting her hand to her chest. "I'm so touched, I can hardly stand it."

We stood watching as the cab made its way down the driveway, turned onto the road and slowly drove away from the nursing home.

About the Author:

Carol Clancy has a Master of Arts degree in English Literature from Cleveland State University. She is currently employed in the business world but has also worked as a teacher, tutor, and, of course, social worker. This is her first novel.